About the Author

From the state of Minnesota in the US.
Career as high school English teacher in southern Minnesota.
Retired to France.

An Atomic Walk into Eternity

Jeff Lien

An Atomic Walk into Eternity

Vanguard Press

VANGUARD PAPERBACK

A CIP catalogue record for this title is available from the British
Library.

ISBN 978 1 80016 668 4

Vanguard Press is an imprint of
Pegasus Elliot Mackenzie Publishers Ltd.
www.pegasuspublishers.com

First Published in 2023

Vanguard Press
Sheraton House Castle Park
Cambridge England

Printed & Bound in Great Britain

Dedication

To Christine and Mathilda

Acknowledgements

Cover art: Christine Pradel Lien
Cover photo: Albert De Boer

The Aveyronnaise

Clare knew what to pack. She had bicycled across Minnesota and Wisconsin, ridden up to Winnipeg, and gone around Lake Superior during the last four summers and had honed her knowledge of what to bring and what to leave behind. Weight and weather were the most important factors; convenience and comfort were secondary. She now used what she had learned from bicycling to prepare for her walk across southern France.

Her clothes were laid out in orderly fashion on the bed: two pairs of light weight hiking pants from which the legs could be detached, four tee shirts, four pairs of heavy socks, underwear, a long sleeve biking jersey, a windbreaker, and a rain poncho. She would need to wash tee shirts, underwear, and socks every few days but could get by with washing the jersey once a week if she did not have to wear it constantly. The jersey with windbreaker would be warm enough for most chilly mountain mornings, if not, she could add the poncho. Her foot gear, a pair of boots and moccasins, lay on the floor next to the bed. She planned to spend most of each day in her boots and use the moccasins only in gites and camps in the evening. On the flight she would stuff the moccasins into her backpack and wear the inelegant boots because they were easier to wear than carry.

Did she need any other gear? Yes, she did, a hat and hiking sticks. Neither her big sun hat nor baseball cap would do. She needed something simple and foldable that protected the back of her neck as well as her face from rain and sun. The sticks had to be light and telescopic so they could be put into the backpack while traveling. She would buy these items later in the day.

She had made her choice of camping equipment long ago. For her first summer of bicycle camping, she used a lightweight, one-person tent, but one morning, as she was trying to put on a sock while standing on one foot, she fell on top of the tent, broke two fiber rods and ripped the fabric. She made do with that tent until returning from her trip, bought a new one, a little sturdier and larger, and thereafter made sure to sit on the ground or to stand clear of the tent when putting on her socks.

While her sleeping bag was not particularly warm, it had kept her comfortable during fifty-degree summer nights in Minnesota and slightly cooler nights along the Canadian coast of Lake Superior. By the internet she had discovered that, other than the Alps and the Pyrenees, the city of Aurillac, just thirty or forty miles north of the trail, often had the lowest temperatures in France, but since the trail's summer temperatures were comparable to those of Minnesota, the bag would suffice.

She could not sleep well without a pillow. Bundling up smelly socks, a sweaty tee shirt, and her jacket to make a pillow didn't work. Both the smell of the pile and the need to re-stack it during the night kept her from sleeping well. After two summers of camping, she finally bought a foam tube covered with cloth to use as a pillow. Sixteen inches long and ten inches in diameter, it fitted on the back of her bike and could be hung as easily on her backpack.

Being a bicyclist, she did not own a backpack and had to buy one. Wanting something lightweight but durable, she went to a shop specializing in hiking equipment and bought an expensive pack with a quilted belt that distributed weight evenly on her shoulders and hips. It was large enough to hold her clothing and had space on top to set a folded tent, sleeping bag, and rolled mattress. On the sides were places to hang a water bottle and the pillow.

Every item but one had now been accounted for. She pulled open the bottom drawer of her dresser and from behind a pile of faded, well-worn jeans withdrew a large jackknife. She held the knife in her open palm for a moment, scrutinizing its gray, desiccated wooden handle. Once belonging to a World War One foot soldier, it had a blade at one end that folded into the handle and a spoon at the opposite end that folded along the handle. It reminded her of an industrial age machine, inelegant and clunky, hardly like a modern military knife, and it would have fitted nicely with threshing machines, hay wagons, and horses. Despite its weighty awkwardness, she had taken it on bicycle trips because it was handy for tasks such as opening cans, spooning out beans, and cutting saplings.

She remembered how the knife had come to her. It had lain forgotten and unused in an old cigar box in her parents' San Francisco home for decades. While she and her mother were cleaning the basement one spring, her mother found the box in a closet, pulled it off the shelf, and handed it to her, saying, "Take this."

Opening the box and seeing the relic, Clare had asked, "What's this for?"

"This knife has been in the family for almost a century," her mother replied. "Your great grandmother Adele kept it as a memento of an American soldier when she came to America. It's a reminder of our American roots in France. I want you to keep it."

"What are you talking about? I don't understand American roots in France. How could we have American roots in France? I thought we had French roots in France."

"Your great grandmother knew the American who carried this knife in the war."

"I don't understand. Which war?"

"They met during World War One in eastern France."

"Didn't Great Grandmother Adele live in Aveyron on the southwestern side of France?"

Sensing Clare's annoyance and frustration, her mother said, "Sit down, and I'll explain."

Clare settled on the sofa, and her mother began. "Years ago, your father and I hiked across the region where your great grandmother was born and raised. The landscape was rugged, the fields and pastures stony and dry. When Adele was young, this region was a poor, isolated backwater, religious and conservative. There were no railway lines and few modern roads. Infant mortality and illiteracy rates were high, and government administrators in the department were known for draft dodging and corruption. Her family made a meager living by raising sheep and goats, planting garden crops among the stones, and harvesting nut and fruit trees.

"Despite this poverty your great grandmother was a hardworking student known in the community for her intelligence. She sucked up information like whales feeding on krill in the Bay. When finishing high school though, she had few prospects. In fact, she had only two. One choice was to marry a man from the community, probably a farmer or village merchant, and raise a family in Aveyron; the other was to become a nun and work in the Church. Not wanting to marry and stay in that hard, stony land, she left her family and traveled across France to enter a convent in the east. The year was 1913.

"Not long after her arrival, World War One started and fighting broke out in the region. Since the convent was in a village near the trenches, it was turned into a makeshift hospital, and the sisters became attendants and assistants to battlefield nurses and doctors. One afternoon a wounded American soldier was brought into the convent. I remember your great grandmother's vivid description of the day. Cannons fired almost continuously, but when there was a lull in the bombardment, she could hear soldiers cursing and screaming in the distance. Pastures in the hills smoldered and burned, set ablaze by shells and bombs gone astray. On days of heaviest fighting, smoke drifted lazily into the village as though it wanted to be contrary to all the surrounding turmoil and engulfed trees in a haze that turned them into shimmering ghosts. It was on one of these days the American was pulled from a weary, gray ambulance, carried by stretcher through the haze into the convent, and laid on a bed.

"Your great grandmother's first task was to help a nurse cut off the soldier's bloody uniform. As they worked, an object fell out of the soldier's pocket and slid into the shadows under the bed, unnoticed in the rush of the moment. She helped bathe the soldier and dress his wounds, and after that could do little but feed and comfort him. She spoke no English and he no French, and in the few days that followed, their only communication was through her attentive care, his incoherent murmurs of gratitude, and the expression of thankfulness in his eyes. When he slept, she stopped at his bed from time to time to study his face. Covered with a ragged beard and disfigured by pain and fatigue, it gave little indication of age. He could have been twenty or thirty or more.

"Raised in poverty and living in a war zone, she had become a hardened, durable woman, but neither austerity of poverty nor brutality of war could suppress a sympathetic, perhaps romantic curiosity that began to grow in her as she cared for this man. Setting aside her vows to the Lord, she allowed herself to muse about him. His face was so unlike those of the brown eyed, black bearded, tough Aveyronnais farmers and the war-weary fighters. Was he like them, she asked herself. Did he come from a place like Aveyron, where work, religion, and politics repressed and hardened men, or did he come from a place green and fertile where men were refined and affable? She wanted to know him.

"A few days later he died. His body was put into a wooden box, his few belongings stuffed into a bag, and he was taken away in the same weary, gray ambulance that had brought him. He left as unceremoniously as he had arrived, and that was the end of the encounter. The nascent bond between her and the soldier had been terminated by death. There was, however, a wistful filament of curiosity that remained floating in her mind, and the next morning, as she stripped off the sheets and mopped around the bed that had been his, she wondered what might happen to him now. Would he be laid in a common burial ground and forgotten, or would he be taken to an American cemetery and buried with ceremony and honor?

"As she ruminated about this man, whose blue eyes had been so haunting and evocative, she heard an object slide across the floor under her mop. She knelt on one knee, slid her hand into the shadows under the bed, and pulled out the object. It was a knife belonging to the American. She turned it over in her hands and studied it. It had a polished, dark wooden handle with a spoon-like blade at one end and a shiny cutting blade at the other. The initials C.S.E. had been carved meticulously into the handle. She stood up, dropped the knife into her apron pocket, and continued mopping. Later in the morning when time permitted, she went to the admitting nurse and asked about the American. He was a soldier from a Minnesota regiment, and his name was Carl S. Enderson. That was all the nurse knew about him."

"So now you know how this knife came into the family," concluded Clare's mother.

"And you want me to take it to Minnesota when I leave?"

"I want you to keep it as a remembrance. It was this unknown Minnesota soldier who, in a way, urged Adele to go to America, and he is why you are an American."

"A knife is a peculiar memento to give to a daughter. A bracelet or ring belonging to Great Grandma would be more appropriate, don't you think?"

"Clare, you have her name as your second name, and you are much like her, imaginative, idealistic, and adventurous. I know it's not a girlish gift, but it fits you."

"Well, okay, Mom, thanks for the keepsake. I'll take care of it."

With that half-hearted promise Clare threw the knife into her suitcase and left for Minnesota that summer to begin science studies at the university. Since the day it was given to her, almost ten years before, the knife had lost what little value it had as a memento but gained value as a camping tool. She laid it on the bed next to her socks.

During the afternoon she bought a hat and hiking sticks and the next day took a taxi to the Minneapolis-Saint Paul Airport. At the counter she showed her passport, picked up a boarding pass, and after retrieving her novel, set her backpack on a conveyor. She climbed the stairway to the second floor, laid the book and the contents of her pockets in a tray and passed through a scanner. On the other side she retrieved her things, walked past a restaurant and souvenir shop, and found a seat overlooking the runway.

While waiting for her flight, she opened her book and began reading. Two years earlier on the ride to Winnipeg she had started reading to fill time while resting or waiting for sleep. For that trip she had been inclined to pick a novel by an Icelandic author, whose mysteries were dark and brooding, but thought that since she would be bicycling cross country, a road book might be more appropriate. She could have shopped on the internet but preferring to hold books in her hands, went to a nearby Barnes and Noble store and sauntered through the novel section. Hoping to find something like Steinbeck's *Travels with Charlie,* one of her favorite books, she settled on *Travels with a Donkey in the Cevennes* by Robert Louis Stevenson, who wrote about the people he met, the land he crossed, and Modestine, his stubborn donkey, while hiking through the mountains of southern France toward the Mediterranean in 1878.

Wanting something more modern for her ride around Lake Superior the following summer, she picked Jack Kerouac's *On the Road*, a book that inspired Steinbeck when he wrote *Travels with Charlie*, but which was quite different. In the nineteen days it took to bike around the lake she read Kerouac from cover to cover. At first it was difficult to get into the story because she found his common style of writing irritating. But after reading a few chapters, she discovered occasional elegance in rhythm and imagery, and the language became less irritating when she realized the style of writing mirrored the messy lives of the novel's characters: alcoholic, drug- abusing young men who bummed rides, met friends, made faithless love, and took Greyhounds across the country from East Coast to West Coast.

She had mixed emotions about Sal, the narrator in *On the Road*. She felt a closeness to him because of his innocent and naive search for a state of mind the beatniks called "It", but she was put off by his self-indulgent lifestyle. An aspiring writer, he had hitchhiked into what he thought would be a deliriously exciting American West, carousing and writing with friends in Denver then moving on to San Francisco, the center of the 1950s beat culture. In San Francisco he became fascinated with black musicians, thinking he could find the enlightenment of the "It" in their music, but neither in the city nor on the road did he find this elusive state for himself, and he returned to the east, rootless and unfulfilled. Eventually he left the east and crossed the country a second and third time, always looking for a Zen-like tranquility in the self-indulgence of the road.

For her hike across France, she chose Robert Pirsig's novel *Zen and the Art of Motorcycle Maintenance*, assuming it also was a road adventure and curious about the strange juxtaposition of the themes of art, mechanics, and Zen. She had started the book in the Barnes and Noble cafe and read just enough to discover it was about a motorcycle trip west from Minneapolis by a married couple on one cycle and a philosophic narrator and his young son on the other. She looked forward to descriptions of western landscapes from the viewpoint of a traveler on two wheels.

She read until the noise of jet engines muffled by thick terminal windows drew her attention away from Pirsig to an airliner moving past. Looking up just as the plane began its slow and heavy rise, she watched it tilt gently upward and disappear beyond the window frame. She closed her book, set it next to her on the bench, and thought about the passengers on the flight, imagining their eager anticipation of what lay ahead.

Only a day away from France, she too was pleased to be on her way, but she had not yet separated entirely from her work. One issue in particular was still on her mind. A high school science teacher, she had started an apiary in an orchard behind her school, and with the project now in its third summer, had risked putting its maintenance into the hands of her students. Her juniors and seniors had promised to manage the apiary while she was gone, but she was not entirely confident in their ability to follow the schedule laid out for them. Honeybees didn't need close attention, but they needed regular attention. When the top box of a hive was almost full of honey, another box had to be added, and if this were not done in a timely manner, the colony would abandon the hive on a sunny summer noon and fly to a more spacious place to resettle.

She remembered following an escaping swarm with her car during her first summer of beekeeping. Luckily, it flew only a couple of miles and landed near the road on a low hanging tree branch. She set a new hive box under the branch, shook the queen and a few workers into it, put the top cover on, and made sure the entrance at the bottom was open. Then hoping all the workers would join the queen in the box by nightfall, she left. Early the next morning before the workers began foraging, she returned to plug the entrance and bring the box filled with bees back to the apiary. With the memory of this escapade in mind, she required students to check hives for animal or human tampering and honey production twice a week. If everything went well, each hive would contain twenty-five or more pounds of honey to be extracted and sold at the end of the season, and students would have learned much about nature and responsibility.

Beekeeping was an unusual component of a high school curriculum even in science classes, but she was curious about how nature did its work and was always looking for ways to keep her biology students involved in learning. She hadn't started her career with a plan to teach beekeeping, but the idea took hold and crept into her curriculum when she discovered how interesting and useful the craft could be. She bought hive kits early one winter, swarms the following spring, and the project began. Most students were willing to study the development of a bee and a hive if explanations were not excessively detailed. Her restless students liked constructing the stands, boxes, and covers, and some, because of their reckless nature, were daring enough to insert swarms into the hives in the spring. Others were interested in applying medications and drugs that protected bees throughout their yearly cycle, and a few even agreed to talk about bees and give demonstrations in a nearby retirement home. Everyone wanted to extract and bottle honey in the fall because sales at local grocery stores brought in hundreds of dollars, some of which was used for a rather sumptuous class party just before Christmas vacation.

Early in her career while teaching in a little town along the western border of Minnesota, she discovered beekeeping because of an interest in athletics. Tall and physically tough, she played basketball with the high school girls during the winter and became their assistant coach for softball in the spring. The softball diamond was several blocks from the school just beyond a small neighborhood. While walking through this neighborhood on her way to practice one afternoon, she noticed a box covered with bees. Never having seen a hive up close, she stopped to look at it from the safety of the sidewalk, and noticing an old man sitting on the front steps of the house next to which the hive stood, she inquired about it. He said he was the keeper and invited her to stop and chat.

On weekends when she had time and students were gone, she sat on the old man's steps and while drinking a

Schlitz with him, listened to his discourse on bees as they watched them work. On hot summer days when the front of the hive was black with bees, she was reminded of a busy airport. As foragers flew away in search of flowers, others returned like cargo transports lumbering toward the hive entrance at the bottom, their leg pockets full and the hair on their bodies sprinkled with yellow, orange, or red pollen depending on their choice of flower. At first she saw just a jumbled mass of flying bugs, but when learning how organized a hive was and how disciplined each bee had to be, she began to think of it as an extraordinary organism engrossed in a singular effort. It was then that she decided to become a beekeeper and teach the craft of beekeeping to her students.

The Flight

Boarding started at 5:.45 p.m.. She found seat thirty-one f, and having no carry-on luggage except her book, sat down, snapped on her seat belt, and turned to look out the window. As she watched workers with large yellow ear-protectors hanging around their necks load baggage into a neighboring plane, a woman stuffed a small bag into the overhead compartment and dropped into the seat next to her. After sliding a laptop computer under the seat and fastening her seat belt, she turned to Clare and cheerfully introduced herself as a scientist studying the aging process in fruit flies. Clare introduced herself as a high school science teacher who managed an apiary with her students, but before she could say little more, the revelation that she was a beekeeper impelled the scientist to launch into an unexpected treatise on her research. Using gene manipulation and food reduction, she had found a way to lengthen the lives of fruit flies. To illustrate her work, she pulled a sheaf of documents from the laptop case, and encouraged by Clare's expressions of curiosity and attentive murmurs, explained the details of her research, using complex graphs and charts. The scientist had picked a good listener. Clare became engrossed in the study and began thinking about how the same principles could be applied to honeybees.

The conversation was interrupted when a hostess moved down the aisle checking to make sure seat belts were fastened. Moments later, the plane was backed onto the runway and the flight began. The scientist waited patiently until she could be heard over the roar of the engines then finished her lecture by saying she was going to Norway to present her results to a group of international scientists on a cruise ship in the fjords. She slid her charts and graphs back into the laptop case and said, "Enough about my research, interesting as it may be. Are you traveling for work or pleasure? If you are a high school teacher, I assume you are on summer vacation."

"I'm planning to walk west across southern France this summer and across Spain next summer."

"Oh, that's exciting. I've heard France has lots of hiking trails."

"Yes, you can walk just about any place on a trail in France. Villages are not far apart and it's fairly easy to find good places to eat and stay."

"I assume you speak French."

"Yes, I do. My great grandmother was a French native who immigrated to San Francisco. I learned to speak the language at home with my grandmother and mother, and I also studied it in high school and college."

"Do you have your route planned or are you just going to ramble around like some of my friends did in Italy when we were in college?"

"I am going to hike a trail to the western tip of Spain just beyond the city of Santiago, where a shrine to Saint James is located. In France, this trail is called Grande Randonnée 65 or GR 65 in abbreviated form."

"Trails with numbers don't sound interesting to me. Does this trail have a name?"

"Yes, it does. In fact, it has several names. The name in French is Le Chemin de Saint Jacques de Compostelle, and in Spanish it's El Camino de Santiago de Compostela. Most Americans don't know about the trail, but I suppose those who do, call it The Trail to the Shrine of Saint James."

With the persistent curiosity of a researcher, the scientist continued. "I know that chemin and camino mean 'trail' or "road", but what does compostelle mean?"

"It's a Latin word. Compo means 'camp', and stelle means 'star'."

"So Compostelle must have been a camp of some kind under the stars. What does a camp under the stars have to do with Saint James?"

"The camp was on a prairie that became a battlefield more than once in the history of the region. The Romans fought local tribes there, and centuries later Christians fought Moors or Muslims in the same place. In Roman mythology soldiers camped on this prairie before a battle, and as they bedded down, a soldier poet looked into the sky and fashioned a poem about stars and death in war. The next day the prairie became a bloody battleground, and by the end of the day it was scattered with bodies of both

Roman soldiers and tribal fighters. In the long conflict against the Moors, the Apostle James was chosen to be the mythical leader and inspiration of the Christians. After the Moors were driven out of the region, the Cathedral of Santiago was erected on this battleground to honor him, and it has been a destination of hikers ever since."

"This walk of yours seems like a big adventure. How long is it going to take?"

"Oh, I won't finish it this summer. I have to be back to school by mid-August. I figure I can walk fifteen miles a day and maybe make nine hundred miles at best."

"That's pretty ambitious. I could probably walk five miles a day but not fifteen."

"People have taken these trails to the Atlantic for thousands of years. Walking them is not unusual. I've even heard about an eighty-year-old Norwegian woman walking it."

"I might be able to keep up with an eighty-year-old."

"Walking a certain distance each day is not a strict goal for most hikers because they have different reasons for being on the trail. I've heard about people taking the trail several times and writing books about their observations and sentiments. Some hikers walk to explore the land and meet people; others walk to the shrine to express their faith."

"What is it for you? Are you an adventurous hiker or a religious pilgrim?"

"I think of myself as an adventurer with the disposition of a first walker."

"First walker. That's a curious description. What's a first walker?"

"First walkers, as I imagine them, were the people who created these trails to the Atlantic long before the Romans and Christians. They walked to the edge of what is now Spain to venerate the sun as it set on the ocean horizon. To them the sun was powerful, life-giving, and mysterious. They came to the shore with no formal religion, and their veneration of the sun was naïve, pure, and simple."

"These early walkers you're talking about remind me of Native Americans."

"Yes, I suppose you could say that. I like to believe the first walkers, like Native Americans, lived in harmony with nature. I want to walk to the Atlantic and see the sun set as the first walkers did."

"I suppose you'll meet some of your relatives while in France."

"I'll be walking through the Averyon, the department where my great grandmother came from, but I doubt meeting any family. We lost contact with French relatives long ago."

By now the plane was above the western shore of Lake Superior, and its angle of ascent was flattening to a gentle climb. Passengers had taken off their seat belts, and hostesses were making their way up the aisles with beverage carts. During a pause in conversation Clare glanced out the window and was surprised to recognize the western shoreline of Lake Superior and the highway she had taken on her bicycle trip. From the plane's altitude, the road below looked narrow and remote, but she knew this view was deceptive. Along the way she had stopped at cafes, pie shops, and fish markets, talked to residents, tourists, and bicyclists, and seen ships and boats moving back and forth on the lake as though they were on the sea.

"What group are you with?" asked the scientist.

"I'm not with a group. I'm going alone."

"You plan to walk nine hundred miles by yourself! Isn't walking alone dangerous for a woman?"

"No, not particularly. Walking alone is common on the trail. There are always walkers going one way or the other, and a single walker is rarely far from others."

"I could imagine some romantic Frenchman or Romanian or some guy from somewhere coming up to you and asking to walk with you. Then one thing leads to another."

"There is a certain etiquette that people on the trail follow, but if a guy forgets his manners, I'd just tell him to kiss off, and I'd keep walking."

"Some men aren't that easy to get rid of."

When the hostess arrived, Clare and the scientist ordered sodas, chatted a few minutes more, then turned to their own interests. The scientist pulled out her speech to do a final edit, Clare opened her novel to read, and they worked until dinner. After dinner, the cabin lights were turned down, and passengers prepared for the night. The scientist turned off her overhead light, tilted the seat back, and covered herself with a blanket. Clare said good night, turned off her own light, and searched unsuccessfully for a movie.

Although the plane was heading east into deep night, the evening was still early, and unable to sleep, Clare thought about the road along Lake Superior over which the flight had passed. She remembered lying in her tent near the road listening to animals of the forest, being startled by the throaty screech of a large bird nearby, and amused by a little creature who scratched on the outside of her tent. When she scratched on the inside in response, it squealed and quickly scurried away through the dry leaves.

She began her ride around Superior at Two Harbors just north of Duluth, and camping every sixty five to seventy miles, had followed the shoreline north north-east through Beaver Bay, Grand Marais, and other towns, some picturesque, some industrial. At Grand Portage she stopped to show her passport, feeling small and insignificant standing next to her loaded bicycle in a long line of cars and semi-trailer trucks inching their way to the check point.

Beyond Grand Portage she continued northeast until coming to Thunder Bay, a city that held a monument to Terry Fox, a Canadian hero, whom she admired greatly. Wanting to visit his memorial, she stopped at a cafe along the road to buy a cup of coffee and ask for directions. When finishing her break, she went to the cashier, handed him a five-dollar bill, and asked how to get to the memorial. He gave her directions, then while holding her change, described the life of the young man in detail as if

Clare were an uninformed tourist. Fox was a young athlete who lost his leg to cancer and then ran with a prosthetic leg from Saint John's, Newfoundland, on the Atlantic coast to Thunder Bay, halfway across Canada, where the cancer returned, stopped his run, and eventually ended his life. When the cashier finished his story, he handed her the change, and she thanked him for his helpfulness and left.

At the monument she leaned her bicycle against a tree and approached diffidently, as though she were meeting the hero himself. The statue stood on a pale purple granite base, which rested on a pedestal formed like a section of an arched bridge. As though he were running, Fox's muscular left leg was placed before the thin, seemingly fragile, artificial one. His head, covered with curly hair and supported by a thick, muscular neck, was turned skyward. Gazing at the statue, she thought about Fox's courage and amazing physical drive. At first she had admired him, but as she grew and matured, he had drifted into her psyche and taken a permanent place within. She then came to see his stubborn and unfettered spirit in a different light, and he became symbolic as well as heroic.

Beyond Thunder Bay she cycled through Fort William, Port Arthur, and Nipigon, following the eastern curve of the lake toward its northern end. From the start of the trip the weather had been cool and clear, good for riding, but now it began to rain. Passing through a small town in a light drizzle, she spotted three loaded bicycles leaning against the wall of a cafe and stopped for a break. Entering the cafe, she sat down at a horseshoe-shaped counter opposite the owners of the bicycles, ordered a berry pie and coffee, and began to chat. The cyclists were college students crossing Canada from west to east. They had climbed the Rockies, crossed the Great Plains, and were looking forward to the Great Lakes. When finishing their break, they said goodbye, wished her good luck and left, intent on the day's ride.

In no hurry to have riding companions, especially three randy college boys, she browsed through a local newspaper lying on the counter and ate pie at a leisurely pace. When she'd finished, she put on rain gear, stopped at a grocery store to buy food, then rode through the day until coming to a small campground where a cement block building with toilets and showers enticed her to turn in for the night. The next day she began in the same intermittent light rain and continued northeast until rounding the northern tip of the lake and turning south. When she got up the following morning, the sky was sunny, and a light wind came from the north northeast. Figuring she could make good time with a breeze at her back, she decamped hastily and started off, snacking as she went. About mid-morning she began losing energy due to an inadequate breakfast, and when coming to a cafe across the highway from a tranquil bay, she pulled in.

"What can I get for you this morning, young lady?" asked the man behind the counter.

"I'll have two fried eggs, hash browns, toast, orange juice, and cup of plain yogurt," Clare responded.

When he came with her order a few minutes later, the waiter asked, "How far you going?"

"I'm going around the lake."

"You camping?"

"Yah. Canada is much better for camping than Minnesota. It's much easier to find sites here. You can stop almost anywhere, walk into the woods, and set up camp. Hard to do that in Minnesota."

"I get fishermen up here from Minnesota every winter. I set fish houses out on the lake and rent them by the day or the week. A lot of them stay at my motel. By the way, if you're camping, be careful of the moose."

"Why is that? I thought bears were the dangerous ones."

"Bears tend to mind their own business, but moose are erratic. You never know what they'll do. They might attack at any time, and at twelve-hundred pounds they can do a lot of damage. If you see one, just leave the area, no questions asked."

Clare ate breakfast and read the local newspaper, looking from time to time out the window to see if a rampaging moose were charging across the road toward the cafe. She cleaned up the remainder of her eggs with the last of the toast, drained her glass of juice, then went to pay her bill.

"You've got three tough hills to climb this morning," her waiter said as he handed her change, "but you should be out of them by early afternoon."

She walked out to her bike, checked to see that the tires were firm, and started off. The waiter was entirely correct, for by the time she had climbed the third hill, her back and thighs were aching. Seeing a large boulder near the edge of the highway at the top of the third hill, she pulled over and climbed up on it to rest and absorb the afternoon sun.

She hadn't been sat there long, however, when one of the college bicyclists panted up the hill. Seeing her, he stopped and leaned his bike against the boulder next to hers. She was not at all pleased to see him. During their cafe conversation he had reminded her of a Spanish bullfighter who strutted and preened as though a thousand admiring countrymen were watching. His manner had been as slick and greasy as his thick black hair. She suspected his companions had ditched him.

"I see you made it up the hills," he said. "When did you start?"

"I don't know, I suppose about ten," she replied, her voice expressionless.

"You made better time than me."

"My bike has low gears. I could climb a wall with it."

"My name is Xavier. I started out in BC with a buddy, but he couldn't take the rain and mountains, so he quit like a whipped pup and went back home on the train. Me, I kept going."

"I thought you were with those other two bikers."

"I was until they abandoned me. So now I'm riding by myself."

She could understand why they had left him and was pleased that the boulder was too small for both of them and high enough for her to look down on him.

"How far you going?" she asked, hoping he would leave soon.

"The Atlantic Coast, I don't know where exactly. I just want to see the coast. Then I'll take a train back to BC."

"Why are you going south when the Atlantic is east of here?"

"I don't want to take a northern route. Places to get food are too far apart, it might be a long push if I break down, and I want to see what it's like around the Great Lakes."

She hadn't rested as long as she wanted, but annoyed and impatient, decided to move on. Slipping off the rock, she mounted her bike and with hardly a look back said, "It's time for me to go."

Irritatingly, the bullfighter followed. For a mile or two he rode behind, hardly saying anything but, she thought, probably admiring her ass. She was not pleased with this ploy.

"My father is Canadian," he said when finally deciding to pull up beside her. "My mother is Brazilian. I inherited my extroverted nature from her. Canadians are rather stuffy. I'm studying business at a school in Vancouver. When I get time, I bike. Keeps me toned."

"This is your first long bike ride?"

"No, I camped with one of my girlfriends last summer. We did a hundred miles down the Pacific coast toward

Seattle. The beach is a nice place to camp. You can gather driftwood, make a fire, and have a good time. A blanket on the sand is a nice place to make love."

Hoping the bullfighter might want to stop to eat, Clare kept riding, nibbling on the few snacks remaining in her handlebar bag. When he didn't drop off, she was forced to endure a long afternoon of stories about his romantic exploits and advice on how to handle her finances, which was a little more interesting than his love conquests. By late afternoon she had lost energy and had to stop. Seeing a cafe near the road, she pulled up and without a word leaned her bike against a wall and walked in. He did likewise.

"What would you like?" the waiter asked with an amusing Canadian French accent.

The bullfighter ordered a buttery gratin of potatoes, leeks, and ham. Curious about Canadian food, Clare ordered a large dish of poutine. When their plates arrived, she turned a bit of the poutine over with her fork and wished she had asked about it before ordering. On her plate was a concoction of cheese, French fries, and brown gravy, all mixed together. Even before tasting it she decided never to order poutine again. After dinner she and her adhesive partner got back on their bicycles and rode until the sun began to set. By now she was resigned to having a camping partner and when coming to a suitable site, resolutely pulled in. She set her tent up as far as possible from the bullfighter's, making sure the opening was on the far side.

"Let's make a campfire," he said.

She never made fires while camping and didn't want to start one now. Thinking a cozy fire was his first step to making love, she said, "No, I'm going to read until the sun goes down," and without another word, crawled into her tent and zipped the opening closed. She lay on top of the sleeping bag, adjusted her pillow, and without taking her clothes off read Kerouac until the light faded.

The bullfighter stayed in his tent that night, but she knew he would soon come calling. She got up early the next morning hoping to leave unnoticed, but he was already awake. They rode together through the day until coming to Michipicoten, where they found a church that offered free rooms to hikers and bikers for the night. After supper she went directly to her room, washed socks and underwear in the sink, then showered and went to bed. The next morning, she left alone at sunup and rode south to Sault St. Marie, a distance which she doubted he could ride in a day. There she found an RV camp ground and happily put up her tent between two gigantic, well-worn, dirty motor homes just returned from Alaska.

Arriving in France, Clare was awakened by the sun shining through cabin windows and the sounds of hostesses serving breakfast. The scientist was wide awake and waiting patiently with her tray down. "Sleep well?" she asked.

"Yes, I did," replied Clare, "although I dreamt about bears and moose on the trail. You might see an occasional boar or deer but probably not a bear or moose. How about you?"

"I slept well enough, except when I dreamt about being on the fjords. I don't know if it was the cold, deep water or my presentation that agitated me more."

After breakfast, the captain announced that the descent into Keflavik, Clare's stopover on the way to France, had begun, and half an hour later the plane crossed low over the coastline with the airport in sight. Studying the landscape through her window, she was reminded how dissimilar Minnesota and Iceland are in climate and topography. Mid-continent Minnesota is a land of extreme heat and cold, while Iceland, near the Arctic Circle, is a land of cold weather mitigated by the sea. And whereas Minnesota has prairie to the south and forests to the north, Iceland has warm pools, bogs, and crags in the south, and tundra, penetrated by fjords, in the north.

The absence of tall trees on the Icelandic landscape brought to mind her Viking ancestors. When they arrived near the end of the first millennium, a long warm period had begun, and trees were relatively abundant. But when the warm period ended, the climate returned to its former, unsympathetic self, and where trees, cut down to build houses, sheds, and ships once grew, there were now only shrubs and bushes with occasional stands of willow and birch.

"What do you do when you get lost in a forest in Iceland?" Clare asked the scientist.

"I don't know. What do you do?"

"You stand up."

Leaning over Clare and looking out the window, the scientist said, "Now that I see the landscape, I can understand the significance of that joke."

Passengers disembarked and entered the terminal. Wishing her good luck, the scientist said goodbye and left to find her flight to Norway, and Clare ambled off to buy a mid-morning coffee in the terminal cafe. She listened to passing airport workers converse in Icelandic and English, switching easily back and forth from one language to the other and watched tourists browsing through colorful sweaters, woolen blankets, jewelry, and souvenirs in shops across the way. She noted that Icelanders tended to be blue eyed and fair haired like Minnesota Scandinavians. A stereotype of Minnesota Scandinavians is that they are friendly but a little distant, an attitude termed "Minnesota nice." She wondered if Icelanders had a similar mindset.

When her flight was announced, she climbed the stairs with fellow passengers, passed through customs and found her seat again next to a window. Soon the plane was airborne, heading south toward the continent, and a couple hours later it passed over the green and black, disorderly fields of northern France to land at crowded Charles de Gaulle. Having shown her passport at customs in Keflavik, she lifted her backpack off the conveyor, walked out of the airport, and took a bus to Gare Montparnasse, where she climbed into a magnificent but dirty TGV and continued going south.

She thought about reading Pirsig but fatigued by travel and hypnotized by the rhythmic motion of the train, she soon fell asleep and did not wake up until hearing the announcement of arrival at Gare de Lyon Part-Dieu. At Lyon she transferred to a slower, regional train that lumbered lazily through mountain passes and tunnels toward Le Puy-en-Velay, a city of forty-thousand inhabitants. She had never been to Le Puy, but having read Stevenson's book about his adventures in the region, the land seemed vaguely familiar.

At Le Puy she got off the train, happy to be out of confinement, and set out to find Les Gites des Capucins. At the office she signed in then went to the sleeping quarters. When making her reservation a month earlier, she had expected something like a hotel room, but what she got was a bed in a dormitory with a toilet and shower. A sign on the door forbade setting backpacks on beds, so she laid her pack on the floor next to a convenient bed and left to find a restaurant.

She ate a soup of cabbage, pork, and potatoes then returned directly to the gite, fatigued by more than twenty hours of travel. The first to arrive, she cleaned up and went to bed, but unable to sleep in anticipation of other hikers, pulled out Pirsig and read. During the evening her dormitory mates, all men, ambled in. She felt slightly ill at ease acknowledging them from her bed as they arrived, but they did not seem to notice, as though this were routine among hikers. That night she slept well despite being the only woman in the little dormitory.

The next morning, she stopped for tea, orange juice, and a pain au chocolat at a cafe, then left to explore the city. Built among mountains and volcanos, Le Puy seemed tilted and disorderly, its streets twisting and turning without reference to north and south. But while there was little regularity in the layout of the city, the cream-colored walls and orange-tiled rooftops created a comforting harmony. She walked about, glancing in shop windows, skirting outdoor cafe patios, and stepping aside for kids on scooters.

Her exploration was temporarily suspended when she saw a woman across the street sitting on the sidewalk with a paper cup at hand. Studying the woman, apparently a beggar, from a distance, she thought there was something unusual about her. Large and heavy, she did not fit Clare's stereotype of a beggar. But when seeing that the woman was sitting next to a grocery store entrance, she assumed her weight was due to the days, months, or years she had sat inert on the street and to generous people coming out of the grocery store to hand her snacks as well as coins. She expected the woman to look used and dispirited, but saw she had a jovial air about her and was taking a lively interest in people bustling along the street.

A shopper came out of the store with groceries in hand and stopped to chat. The two women were at ease with each other as though they had spoken before, and as they talked, Clare wondered whether the beggar would get cookies or coins. After a few minutes of conversation, the shopper set her groceries down, took coins from her purse, and dropped them into the cup. The beggar grasped her hand, kissed it, and the shopper moved on.

Clare crossed the street and stopped nearby. Ill at ease standing above, she said, "Bonjour, Madame. Comment allez-vous?" To her surprise, the woman returned the greeting with a burst of eager, semi-decipherable chatter that would not allow Clare merely to drop a coin into the cup and move on. Using simple French, hand signs, and another language foreign to Clare, the woman introduced herself, explaining that she came from a country in the east, lived in a gypsy camp, and was now alone because her two children stayed behind, and her husband abandoned her. Communicating in three languages, two of which Clare hardly understood, was exhausting, and during a pause, she pulled a two-euro piece from her pocket and dropped it into the cup. The woman grabbed her hand, kissed it, and said, "Merci, merci, Madame."

"C'était un plaisir de vous rencontrer, Madame. Bonne journée," Clare replied. Then she too walked on, feeling a bit down.

While watching the woman from across the street, Clare had thought of her as a beggar, but after meeting her and learning a little of her history, the word beggar seemed narrow and dehumanizing. She tried other words such as tramp, vagrant, hobo, and pan handler, but none seemed appropriate. Wanting something more gracious, she recalled the poetry of Robert Louis Stevenson. After choosing his novel at the bookstore for her trip to Winnipeg, she moved to books of poetry. While browsing in the poetry section, she was surprised to discover a little collection of Stevenson's poems and paused to read a few about travelers on foot. One poem, charming and hopeful, celebrated the happy liberty of the open road. But others were less optimistic. She recalled two poems in particular. In one a wanderer lamented that he would never be able to return home because it no longer existed, and in the other a wayfarer, apparently near the end of life, looked back on his years, comparing them to climbing and descending slopes.

Her brief reading of Stevenson's poetry prodded her to think of the woman as a wayfarer, not to describe her as a traveler because her territory consisted only of a sidewalk in a small city, but to suggest a history of grief and despair. Putting herself in the woman's place, she thought that boredom would drive her crazy, but when realizing she was looking at the woman from the point of view of someone with an interesting, fruitful job, she decided that boredom would be equivalent to a small hill. Getting food and finding a place to live were steep hills, leaving children and family behind were mountains to climb. The woman must have had unrelenting determination and immense courage.

Marveling at how upbeat and involved she seemed, Clare thought of a scrawny alley cat she had seen skulking around her neighborhood. One morning she found it sitting on the ledge of her window. When she opened the window, it fled in a burst of fear. After seeing it a second time a few days later, she left the window open with a dish of food on the ledge. The cat returned to eat and eventually dropped into the living room. Over several months it calmed down, felt at ease, and took up residence with her. Although calm in her house, it remained wary of strangers and intensely reactive to unusual noises and movements. This intense caution, Clare thought, allowed it to avoid dangers and survive, but must have been stressful. She wondered if the woman, so social and at ease on the street, was in some way affected likewise by her experiences.

Weary of downtown crowds, Clare left the city center looking for serenity and space in the surrounding neighborhoods. She expected to see well-manicured lawns and pleasant gardens in the residential areas, but discovered she could see neither lawn nor garden, and leaving the downtown did not diminish the feeling of density. This oppressiveness did not come from human mass for there were few people moving about, but from the omnipresent gates, walls, hedges, and fences she saw wherever she went. Living on the limitless plains of the Midwest, it seemed to her that nothing in the neighborhoods here was left unbound by these barriers, as if inhabitants wanted to prevent the tax assessor from seeing what they owned, or they needed to fortify themselves against thieves and neighbors.

These impediments reminded her of a family she had visited with her mother in northern France. The family's little backyard, which they called a garden, hardly resembled what she was used to. Surrounding high stone walls hid the lawn, flower beds, and garden from public view, and the family likewise could see no more than the peaks of adjacent houses. Only birds sitting in garden trees and cats making their way on the tops of walls could observe life in the neighborhood.

From the street she saw the spires of the cathedral and wanting to get out of the neighborhoods, she decided to tour the church. With the steeple as her guide, she navigated the narrow streets, found a stairway leading to the cathedral's front door and began to climb. As she mounted the many stone steps, a preview of her climb out of the city the next morning, she thought that attending service must keep members of the congregation in good physical condition if nothing else. She entered the cathedral, awed by the architecture of the building and the skills needed to construct it, and ambled around, inspecting icons and stained-glass windows. At the end of her tour, she stopped at the gift shop to buy a guidebook and a créanciale, a sort of trail passport, which she asked to have stamped. Her first stamp, about two inches square, was an image of the Virgin Mary holding the Baby Jesus, and arching over the two figures were the words Cathédrale de Le Puy-en-Velay. Her walk to Compostelle had now officially begun.

She tucked the document into a pocket, left the cathedral, and returned to the tangled streets below. One shop that attracted her attention was a studio through whose window she had seen samples of white lace, large and small, displayed on bright red walls. She returned to the shop and entered. Near the door was a lace-making machine. Built about the time her military knife had been made, it rattled and shuddered as it produced identical pieces one after another. She watched it toil, marveling at the quality of lace despite its arthritic decrepitude. In the middle of the shop a man sat at a little table weaving a unique piece. Working mechanically, he gazed indifferently at tourists who stood nearby watching his fingers move bobbins back and forth. Like the weaving machine and knife, he was part of an antiquated tradition.

After leaving the lace shop, Clare stopped at the Tam Tam Café in the central square to have a dinner of green lentils, for which Le Puy is famous. While waiting for her order, she opened her guidebook. She had chosen this guide because it had simple maps indicating distances between villages on one page and phone numbers and addresses of places to eat and stay on the opposite.

The content was clear and well arranged, but the intriguing title, "Miam Miam Do Do," was a bit mysterious. In modern French jargon "miam miam" means "yum yum," as in reference to delicious food, and "dodo" means "sleep." Thus, the title seemed quite appropriate as a trail guide, but wanting to know more about its origin, she went to the introduction. "Miam Miam Do Do" came from an abbreviation of the Latin religious phrase "Mi Am Do." According to mythology, a well-known fifteenth century stone cutter, who stuttered so badly he had seven sets of twins, took to the trail intending to cut the phrase "Mi Am Do" into arches and doors of churches, convents, and abbeys to remind travelers to love and serve their lord, but since people constantly mocked him, he perversely changed "Mi Am Do" to "Miam Miam Dodo."

The waiter arrived with a large plate of lentils, a basket of bread, and a glass of wine. Clare had expected a simple dish of green lentils and chopped ham, but what she got was more complex. A large sausage lay in a bed of lentils cooked with onion, garlic, tomato, bell pepper, and white beans, all seasoned with a variety of Mediterranean spices. Encouraged by the pleasant appearance and odor of the dish, she relished the lentils and enjoyed the wine. When she'd finished, she walked back to the dormitory, prepared for bed, and read while a new group of hikers entered.

The next morning, she dressed quietly, left as her dormitory mates were waking, and went to eat breakfast in the gite's cafe. When the waitress arrived, she placed her order then asked, "Could you please explain something to me?"

"Certainly. What would you like to know?"

"This is the Gite des Capucins, but what exactly is a gite?"

"Gites are resting places for hikers. They are usually in houses and barns, but they can also be in old factories, distilleries, and mills that have closed. Some are modern, others rustic, but all have a toilet, shower room, sleeping place, and dining room. The owners, whose residence is separate, usually serve dinner and breakfast, but in some gites travelers must make their own meals. Capucins is unusual because we have a cafe with menu and waiters. If you are walking to Compostelle, you will see all kinds of gites."

When Clare had finished breakfast, she stopped at the counter to pay her bill and have her créanciale stamped and signed for the second time. There were sixty-eight squares on the document, enough to get to Santiago if she walked fifteen to twenty miles a day from gite to gite. But since she planned to camp most of the time, it would be signed and stamped only when she decided to take a break from tenting. This time the image was a circle, and inside the circle were the words Gite des Capucins above the pilgrim's symbolic clam shell.

It was not difficult to find GR 65 since it passed near the gite's entrance. Her first objective of the day was Saint-Christophe-sur-Dolaison, a mountain village about nine hundred feet above Le Puy on the Dolaison River. She left Le Puy and began climbing, now and then turning to look down at the city to measure her progress. Her first break of the day, well before Saint-Christophe, was unplanned. Coming around a sharp bend, she discovered a pair of houses close to the trail. The lawn in front of one had a patio with tables, chairs, and a colorful sign inviting hikers to stop for something to eat and drink. Charmed by this little oasis overlooking the valley, she chose a table and sat down.

There were two hikers sitting at separate tables, a man wearing a Bavarian hat and a woman in worn hiking boots and jeans, who was about to leave. The French habitually say hello and goodbye when entering and leaving a public space. Clare had forgotten this etiquette, and when the woman stopped to greet her, she felt ignorantly rude.

"Bonjour, Madame. It's a beautiful day for walking. Have you been out long?" asked the woman.

"No, this is my first day. I started at Le Puy this morning."

"Then you are a novice. You picked a good day to begin. Are your legs tired yet?"

"Not yet, but it will take me a few days to get into good walking shape."

"Have a good walk," said the hiker as she turned to the trail.

"Thank you," said Clare. "And bonne continuation to you."

Clare bought an Orangina to drink there and a sandwich to eat later, and while drinking her soda, listened to birds in nearby trees and gazed across the mountains and valleys. Presently the man in the Bavarian hat, who had been sitting quietly, said, "Excuse me, Madame, I see you have American hiking gear. Are you from the U.S.?"

"Bonjour, Monsieur. Yes, I am."

"I'm curious about an American tradition. Perhaps you could explain it to me."

"What is that?"

"I know that many Europeans went to America seeking religious freedom."

"That's part of our history and mythology, yes."

"I assume America is a very religious country."

"What makes you think that?" asked Clare, a little surprised.

"'In God we trust' is written on all your money."

Clare was amused by the simplicity of this observation. "The founding fathers thought that belief in God was important, but I don't think they had a particular religion in mind. Their idea was to let people worship as they chose."

Clare was expecting some kind of historical or philosophical comment from the man, but instead his reply was as simple as his observation. "It seems Americans are a rational and pragmatic people."

"They tend to be, but not always."

That response must have satisfied the hiker, for as he got up to leave, he smiled and said, "Perhaps we shall meet again farther down the trail."

"Yes, we might do that," acknowledged Clare. "Bonne route."

Clare finished her Orangina, then she too got up to leave. On her way across the patio, she tried to coax a small, yapping dog to step beyond the threshold of the front door, but when it steadfastly refused to come out, she gave up and got back on the trail.

She crossed the Dolaison, started to climb, and came to a farm with a Gite de France sign hanging on the wall of a barn. Beneath this sign was the word L'Abri, a word she did not know but assumed was the name of the gite. When passing the gate of the residence, she paused to look at a vegetable garden with neat rows of cabbages, carrots, tomatoes, and an overgrown patch of zucchini. She assumed the vegetables were used to feed hikers as well as the owner. Turning away from the gate, she noticed another dog. This one was a herding animal of some kind, quite unlike the yapping mutt that had refused to come out to the patio. Hard at work in the front yard, he was lying flat with his muzzle pressed to the ground, keeping an eye on a stray chicken that had left the herd and now seemed to be wondering whether to flee or stand still. Clare watched the intense psychological interaction, wondering how the chicken planned to get out of that situation, but when neither chicken nor dog showed any inclination to move, she lost patience and walked on.

A few miles beyond L'Abri and farther up the mountain she saw a bearded man in a tattered gray robe making his way down the slope toward her.

"Bonjour, Madame," he said when coming close.

"Bonjour," she replied, noticing a dirty Chuck Taylor tennis shoe sticking out from under the robe.

"Excuse me, Madame, I am a priest who is looking for a gite called L'Abri. Have you passed it on your way?"

"Yes, I have," she responded. Turning and pointing down the trail, she said, "It should take no more than an hour to get there."

"Thank you. God bless you, my child."

She expected the man to start off. Instead, he paused, looked into her eyes, and asked, "Do you have a couple of coins for a priest who is hungry?" She had not anticipated a question of this kind and was annoyed by it. Rather than responding to this supplication, she stepped past him and while doing so, murmured in his ear, "When you arrive at L'Abri, be careful of the fierce dog." Then without looking back she continued up the trail, thinking how different his manner was from that of the woman on the street in Le Puy.

The priest's shoes reminded Clare of her father, who played high school basketball in Chuck Taylors in the 1960's. She remembered him saying that Taylors caused twisted ankles and flattened arches. Fortunately for athletes, they were replaced by better shoes in the 1970s even though they still remain popular with the French public. The priest's inquiry about the gite brought to mind her Lanning grandparents, who lived in western Minnesota during the depression. A railway line went through their town, and even though their house was a half mile from the line and out of sight, vagrants jumped off freight trains and came to the door for something to eat. Her father said that his mother often joked about a railroad grapevine because drifters showed up as though a big red X had been painted on the end of the house.

The trail ascended gently into the mountains, and hiking was relatively easy until it suddenly steepened and turned into a narrow gully full of tree roots and rocks. Since there wasn't an alternate path through the underbrush, she used her walking sticks to keep from sliding off rocks and tripping over roots. About halfway up the gully she was surprised to see a man stepping nimbly from rock to rock coming down toward her, and when he came near, she leaned sharply to one side to let him pass. Farther up the gully she had to fling herself into a bush when a group of all-terrain bicyclists plummeted past her.

Although annoyed, she admired their biking skills and assumed they had grown up in the mountains.

At the top of the climb, the gully disappeared, and the trail levelled out to meander through a dark forest on the plateau. About halfway across the plateau, she set her pack down, took out the sandwich she had bought that morning, and sat against a tree to have lunch. Looking at the rays of sunshine piercing the darkness, and hearing the pleasant chirp of little orange breasted birds, she was happy to be hiking and looked forward to the days and miles to come.

After lunch she descended a gully as steep as the one she had climbed but more constricting and difficult. She doubted that runners and cyclists had ever taken this gully. The rocks and stones upon which she balanced were chiseled and angular, and the roots and bushes bordering the gully on both sides gave little space to bypass obstructions. Her downward progress was slow, slower even than the ascent. When she finally reached the bottom, the trail led her to a village on the Allier River. She lurched on weary legs into the hamlet and near the trail found a bar. Picking a table on the patio under a tree, she dropped into a chair and ordered an Orangina.

The department she was crossing was the Auvergne, a rugged, picturesque land where Gallic tribes had fought Roman soldiers two thousand years before. High above, eagles circled in an aerial waltz. The floating and turning of these majestic birds made her think of a captivatingly romantic folk song inspired by the rugged beauty of the region. She took a sip of soda, put her glass down, and when the song came to her, looked into the mountains and began humming its poignant melody. At first she could recall neither the singer of the song nor its title, but after a few measures they came to her. In her imagination she heard Kiri Te Kanawa singing a melody from the "Chants d'Auvergne," a mountain idyll about handsome shepherds, beautiful shepherdesses, and pristine white sheep. The beauty of the melody and the romanticism of the lyrics took hold of her, and for a few moments she was transported, note by note, measure by measure, into an imaginary life among the pastures and mountains above.

When she could remember no more of the song, Te Kanawa's voice faded away, and as the fantasy of high forests and pastures evaporated into the ether, she drifted back to the present. The mountains and valleys reminded her of her great grandmother Adele, who was a native, born and raised a little farther west. Remembering what her mother had said about the hard Aveyronnais landscape and the rough nature of its inhabitants, she thought that Adele saw nothing pristine and romantic in these hard, gully-cut mountains, and she began to understand why her great grandmother had so earnestly contemplated the face of the dying American and taken his knife from under the empty bed.

Something cool and soft touched her bare leg. Lifting the checkered cloth to look under the table, she discovered an animal quite unlike the pristine creatures in the song she had just been humming. A dog, muscular, short-legged, and flat-faced, who could have been loved only by his master, was sniffing her feet. She put her hand under the table and patted the animal's large, bristly head. When his curiosity about her feet was satisfied, and he had had enough petting, he crawled out from under the table and plopped down along the edge of the patio. He must have imagined himself to be a watchdog, for with one front paw crossed over the other, he lifted his head and judiciously eyed patrons coming and going. He remained at his post only a few minutes, however, for when seeing nothing suspicious or even out of the ordinary, he snapped at a fly buzzing near his nose, yawned twice, then jumped off the patio and sauntered across the street. There he joined a group of people standing on the sidewalk in front of a canoe rental shop listening to the proprietor give last minute instructions on handling their crafts. When the lesson was finished, the rowers shouldered their canoes and descended to the river with the dog ambling behind. Shooting rapids, Clare thought, could only be more pleasant than the gully walking she had done that day.

Three hikers sauntered onto the patio and picked a table nearby. When she heard one of them order a beer in badly mangled French with an Irish accent, she addressed him in English. "You must be British?"

"Can hardly speak a word of French," he said, then indicating a chair at her table, asked, "May I?"

She nodded yes, and he left his companions to sit with her.

"All three of you British?" she asked.

"No, they're French, I'm Irish. They can hardly speak a word of English, just enough to get me by. I met them a couple of days ago and we've been walking together since. Where are you from?"

"I'm from Minnesota in the States."

"You look more French than Scandinavian."

Surprised at his knowledge of Minnesota, she responded, "Not everyone from Minnesota is Scandinavian. I happen to be French, well, half French."

"What's the other half?

"Scandinavian."

"Hah. So, I wasn't that far off, after all."

The Irishman took a long swig of beer and said, "You know, a lot of Irish have Scandinavian ancestry thanks to the Norwegian Vikings. They occupied much of Ireland for a century or two near the end of the first millennium and finally left or blended in with the people who had always lived there."

"Are you a Viking?" asked Clare.

"That I am. My distant, distant ancestors were Vikings, and I've Norwegian genes."

"So, you come from savage stock."

"The Vikings have a ferocious reputation, but they had reason to be fighters."

"I suppose the reason is that they were bloodthirsty barbarians."

"You've seen too many bad American movies about Vikings."

"So, what is that reason?"

“They wanted to trade and explore, of course, but there were also involved in a religious war.”

“A religious war! I had never thought of the Vikings’ two-hundred-and-fifty-year rampage as a religious war.”

“The Scandinavians were considered pagans by the Christians because they worshipped multiple gods such as Thor, Odin, and Freya. Their religion created a rough morality that may seem pitiless by our standards today, but it shaped behavior and promoted a sense of community. It wasn’t any more brutal than Christianity was at that time or is now. Christians wanted to exterminate them, so the Vikings fought back by plundering abbeys and monasteries and attacking villages. They didn’t want anyone messing with their beliefs. You walking far?”

“I hope to get to Saint-Jean-Pied-de-Port. Then I have to go back to work.”

“You hike in the U.S.?”

“No, I bike there.”

“I’ve hiked in Spain and Nepal, and I’ve done the Pacific Crest Trail in the States.”

“What’s that trail like?”

“Oh, it’s about as rugged as the Camino but more difficult.”

“Why is that?”

“The Camino has generated a commercial culture with gites, shops, and cafes that makes walking relatively convenient for hikers and profitable for people living along the trail. That’s not the way it is along the Pacific, where towns are farther apart, and you have to carry more food and equipment because the regional culture is not suited to hikers."

"You're not a sailor like your ancestors, I take it."

"No, I'm not. The common misconception is that Vikings were only sailors, raiders, and traders. They were also farmers, craftsmen, hunters, poets and, of course, boat builders. Anyway, I'm a hiker, not a sailor. I get seasick rather easily. When I'm not hiking in other countries, I go up to the north coast of Ireland and walk. Walking alone on that desolate coast while thinking about my Viking ancestors prepares me for the most miserable of walks."

"Walking along the North Sea would probably appeal to the Scandinavian part of my nature. Maybe I'll do it some day."

Clare finished her Orangina and stood up to leave. "It's time for me to move on. I'm going to explore the little church I saw when coming into the village, then I have to get back on the trail. Thanks for the conversation."

"It was my pleasure," said the Irishman, happy to have spoken to someone in his native language. "Good luck on the road."

Stepping over the dog, who apparently had lost interest in canoeing and returned to his security post, Clare turned toward the church. Like many village churches along the trail this one stood on a hill, and encouraged by the curiosity of a tourist, she approached it as she had the Cathedral in Le Puy. When opening the heavy, weather-beaten door to look in, however, she saw neither icons nor soaring vaults. Instead, she saw dusty rays of light slanting down from grimy, stained-glass windows revealing crooked rows of wooden chairs that led to an altar shrouded in shadows at the far end of the church.

As she peered into this melancholy darkness, the cloak of tourism lifted from her shoulders, and she imagined hearing the ceaseless drone of an imploring priest coming from the depths. Disheartened by an archaic tradition and reluctant to go farther into the church, she stood at the door recalling a grim experience she'd had in the Loire Valley. She and her mother had come to France to stay with friends during a Christmas vacation. Just after the holiday, a lovely old lady, close to the family, died in her sleep, and her funeral was held in a large, unheated, unlit church on a sunless, soggy day. Clare sat in the somber gloom with her mother and host family behind the deceased's two elderly sisters and the demented husband of one of them. There were no other mourners, and the service was as routine, unsympathetic, and dark as death itself.

She went in no farther. Letting the door swing shut, she turned toward the sun and contemplated the flowers and trees in the churchyard, trying to regain a sense of nature and life. When the heat of the sun and the fragrance of the flowers enveloped her, she descended.

Along a wall of the church, a young woman was squatting in the grass, taking photos of something on the foundation. Seeing a backpack lying nearby, Clare became curious about the combination of hiking gear and expensive camera. "Bonjour," she said.

"Bonjour," said the woman without looking up.

"You a photographer?" asked Clare, hoping not to sound too naïve.

The woman snapped a photo, turned to look up at Clare and said, "No, not really. I take photos of anything that interests me. The rocks in this wall have intriguing grains and natural designs."

"So, you must be a hiker."

"Yes, I am. I started in Paris a few weeks ago."

"How has the weather been?"

"It was chilly and wet when I started, but as I go southwest and get farther into the summer, the weather improves. By the time I cross into Spain, it will be sunny and hot."

"You plan to take the northern trail or a southern one?"

"I haven't decided yet, but I think trails in the south will be too hot by the time I get there, so I'll probably take the one along the north coast."

The woman turned back to the wall and took a final photo. "This is a good time of day to take photos. Shadows made by these rough stones add depth to images."

The mention of shadows reminded Clare that she would soon need to find a place to camp. "Where do you camp?" she asked.

"I camp along the trail, but I don't like to be seen from the trail. Thousands of people hike every year, but they aren't all saints. It's good to be vigilant."

The hiker stood up, moved past Clare, and climbed the steps to the door.

"It's dark inside. You probably won't get any good photos."

"I'm not going to take photos of the interior. It's the exterior I like," said the woman as she opened the door and slipped into the shadows.

The click of the latch told Clare it was time to move on. She paused momentarily at the bottom of the steps and stared at the door, wondering what the woman would see in the gloom.

She made her way back to the bar and not finding the Irish hiker and his French friends, ate dinner alone. As she hiked out of the village that evening, a marriage reception was about to start. A noisy, honking parade of friends and family drove past and went up the hill to a reception hall. But instead of stopping there, they turned around in the parking lot, came back down, and went through the village a second time with the same incessant, happy noise. The first time they passed, she stopped to watch and wave, but when they came up the hill the second time, she had walked past the reception hall and was making her way into a quiet countryside.

The Beast of Gévaudan

She climbed over the rock wall along which she had been walking, dropped into a pasture, and lay her backpack on the ground. Near the wall she unrolled her tent, inserted the carbon rods to give it form, and pushed the metal stakes into the rocky ground. When the tent was up, she tossed her sleeping bag, pillow, and mattress into it and went to relieve herself along the fence. After brushing her teeth with water from her bottle, she took off her shoes and socks, careful to set them with her backpack under the tent apron in case of rain. Then looking forward to her first night of sleep on the trail, now dark and quiet, she crawled into the tent and zipped the entrance shut. She began sliding into the sleeping bag, but hesitated, wondering if she should keep her clothes on or take them off. Finally ignoring the words of the photographer and wanting to be liberated from the restraint of dirty, sweaty cloth, she cast caution aside, took everything off and slid in.

Waiting for sleep, she remembered explaining to the scientist on the plane what she had meant by first walkers, and now lying in her tent listening to noises of the mountain night, imagined walking with them. Dressed in heavy, simple clothing, shod with crude sandals, and foraging along the way, they walked west to the sea, driven by admiration of the life-giving sun and a naïve curiosity about the universe, visible and invisible. She did not imagine herself to be one of them, for she was a modern hiker separated from them by millennia, but she had the same intent and reason as they for walking to the sea.

Dawn was chilly and cloudy but rainless. She unzipped her sleeping bag, sat up in the tent, and slipped into her underwear, tee shirt and walking shorts. Then unzipping the entrance, she crawled out, put on her socks, boots, and windbreaker, and went to relieve herself along the wall. When she'd finished, she returned to the tent and started packing. As she bent over to roll up her sleeping bag, she was startled by a voice nearby. Whirling around, she saw a beetle-browed man eyeing her over the rock wall.

"Bonjour, Madame," he said without introducing himself. "I see you are walking the trail."

"Yes, of course," she said in an unsteady voice.

"Which way are you going?" he asked.

"West."

"Then you are going to Santiago."

"Yes, I hope to arrive there and go beyond," she said, more calmly now but wondering how long he had been watching her.

"You are walking by yourself?"

Loath to reveal that fact, she responded hesitantly, "Yes."

"Do you need help with anything?"

"Do I look like I need help?" she said to herself, but to the man, replied, "No, I'm fine. Thank you."

"I am returning from the Shrine of Saint James. Do you have anything to eat for a bishop who has been walking for many days?"

Hoping to get rid of the man, she said, "I have a small bag of food you can have," then pulled a sack of trail mix from her backpack and walked over to the stone fence. When handing it across to him, she noticed his coarse brown robe, sandals, and gnarled wooden staff. Although he dressed like the first walkers, she doubted he had gone beyond Santiago to watch the sun set in the sea.

He opened the package and began eating hungrily.

"Do you know how far L'Abri is from here?" he asked. "I would like to stop there tonight."

Feeling as though she were stuck in some kind of déjà vu time warp, she turned, pointed down the trail and said encouragingly, "It's threequarters of a day from here. You should be there by mid-afternoon."

"God bless you, my child. Everything we do has been ordained by God, and I am thankful."

Then making a sign of the cross, the bishop turned, and while eating Clare's breakfast, started off for L'Abri.

Relieved to see him walk away and regaining her sense of humor, she called out, "When you arrive, be careful of the dog."

There was no response from the man, but she imagined he was smiling to himself about the ease with which he obtained her breakfast. How convenient it was that their meeting on the trail and his getting a free meal had been ordained by God. Was she supposed to feel grateful for being chosen? Disliking this simplistic way of thinking, she asked herself, "Did chance or coincidence have anything to do with this meeting?"

She felt manipulated by the dubious bishop and the penniless priest, and thought it curious that both were looking for L'Abri. Were they expecting free food and a bed? Had God put a red X on the end of the gite barn visible only to them, as though their arrival were intended? The railroad vagabonds who arrived at the Lanning residence during the depression came with no pretense whatsoever, and God's will had nothing to do with their arrival. They were hungry and by the railroad grapevine had found a place to eat.

Glancing at the camp site one last time, she climbed over the wall, and started for the next village. An hour later she entered a neat and picturesque neighborhood of dark stone houses with orange tile rooftops and green shutters. The road crossed the neighborhood, curved sharply downward to the right, and arrived at a river. About halfway down the curve, she stopped, and having been drained of energy for lack of breakfast, sat on a public bench to rest. This bench was so close to the edge of the steep hillside that she had to be careful to keep from sliding off and tumbling down the slope. Far below children were playing games on a distant ball field, and a train slowly skirted the field on the far side, entered a tunnel, and disappeared. When her energy returned, she slid cautiously off the bench and continued. At the river she found a cafe-bar, chose a table under an awning on the sidewalk, and sat down.

The waitress was turning from table to table, villagers were chatting over rolls and coffee, and, although the day was an ordinary weekday, the mood seemed festive. While waiting for her order, Clare saw a tall, bearded man in blue overalls and an oversized, yellow-flowered Hawaiian shirt at the opposite end of the patio. With a cigar in one hand and a glass of rosé in the other, he presided over a table of polite hikers, lifting his cigar to emphasize a point, and pausing from time to time to sip his rosé and glance across the crowd. When he spotted an empty chair at Clare's table, he abruptly left his audience and approached to ask if he could borrow it. When she said she had no need of a second chair, he put the cigar in his mouth and with glass in one hand and chair in the other, made his way back to his listeners to continue his monologue, now while sitting.

After a rather lengthy time, his audience got up to leave, his monologue ended, and he brought the chair back to Clare. She expected him to put it in its place and go away, but he sat down and began to talk again. "This is good country for walking. Too bad the trail doesn't follow the river. There are little ports, dams, and water mills all along it. It's very picturesque." Although annoyed by his sitting down without permission, she responded civilly, "I haven't walked very far yet, but I think the country along the trail is beautiful."

Before she could say another word, he began a story. "My father was a wealthy businessman who wanted to send his children to England for a year to learn English. I was the last kid in the family. Before I could go, we had an economic crisis in the region, and my father didn't have enough money to send me away."

At this point in his story, he paused to pull a box of matches from his shirt pocket, and while Clare wondered if she were hearing the same story told to the hikers, he struck a match and relit his cigar. After a couple of puffs and a sip of rosé, he continued.

"'This morning we have eleven new words to learn.' That's the way my high school English teacher began each lesson. I don't know why he picked eleven words. I think ten or twelve would have been more normal. My father wanted me to study science, but science never really interested me. I decided to be an antique and art dealer. I remember getting a call from a contact in Denmark, who asked me to pick up an expensive vase and bring it to London for auction. So, I went to Copenhagen and picked up the vase. To come back, I took a boat to Scotland. From Glasgow I took a night train south to London. About midnight someone knocked on the door of my compartment. It was police checking to see if I had a bomb. I don't know why they would think I was an Irish bomber when I was a Frenchman coming from Denmark. Anyway, they didn't find anything and went away. When I got to London, I took a taxi to my destination. As I was walking across the square to my appointment, the same thing happened again, but this time the bobbies were a bit more aggressive. I felt a hand grab my right shoulder and another my left, and before I knew it, I was on the pavement. Four bobbies held my arms and legs and a fifth one put his boot on the side of my head. A sixth one took the expensive vase and was carrying it to a vacant place across the square. I suppose he too thought it was a bomb. Luckily, the proprietor of the auction house was looking out the window, waiting for me. He ran out on the square and saved the vase and me along with it."

Clare had been transported into a conflict of religion, war, and politics by this imaginative tale, but knew its teller would remain at her table all day long if she did not leave. When he paused to relight his cigar in anticipation of a new story, she got up. "Sorry," she said, "but I must be off. That was a remarkable story."

"I could tell you many more," he said.

Knowing that "bonne continuation" was not necessary, she said goodbye and went to the bar to pay her bill. By the time she left, he had found a new table of polite hikers, and with a fresh cigar and a full glass of rosé, was presiding over them.

With Saugues as her next destination, she crossed the river and started climbing. About halfway up a long slope, she came to a tiny pilgrims' chapel close to the trail. She thought it peculiar that it had no windows, and the door was padlocked shut. She kept climbing and an hour later turned to look back. The chapel had disappeared amongst the trees, but farther below rooftops of the village on the river were still visible. She wondered if the storyteller, with cigar in one hand and glass of rosé in the other, was still at the cafe.

In the region around Le Puy, pastures lay isolated in mountain forests, but farther west, they shared the land with fields of grain and corn. The trail was wide and sandy, and volcanic rock had transitioned to sandstone and limestone, which farmers had been dragging out of fields for generations and piling along the perimeters to avoid damaging cultivators and plows. The countryside fences created by this timeless practice reminded her of a poem by Robert Frost which questioned the worth of stone fences surrounding an orchard north of Boston, while his neighbor suggested that good fences promoted good relationships. Clare disliked the unnatural, intentional barriers in villages and cities that constrained interactions, but here in the farmland she saw how fences had evolved and how useful they had become.

The trail seemed to generate a sense of relationship among those taking it and those living along it. She had heard a story about a hiker who was exhausted. Someone driving past noticed how laboriously she moved, and stopped to ask if she wanted a ride to her destination. When the woman stubbornly said no, the driver offered to transport her backpack. Wanting to walk every inch of the way, she trustingly handed the pack to the driver, and he drove off. When arriving at her destination, a gite in the next town, she found the pack lying at the foot of a dormitory bed.

Throughout France there is a system of signs painted on rocks, trees, and posts to help hikers find their way. The color of these signs depends on the importance of the trail. A sign for the Grandes Randonnées is made of a horizontal white stripe about an inch wide and ten inches long over a parallel red stripe of the same size. Below, a third horizontal stripe, white and shaped like an L with a point, indicates a turn in the trail, and a red and white X warns of a wrong direction. By wandering off Gr 65 and getting lost Clare experienced firsthand how attentive and gracious inhabitants could be. Not paying attention, she took a wrong turn and went a quarter mile off trail before a perceptive local resident stopped his car and instructed her to turn around and go a different way.

Back on GR 65, she finally arrived at Saugues. Walking down a long, grassy slope toward the village, she saw a large green statue in the distance of a woman with a stick fighting a wolf-like creature. Curious about the significance of the statue, she paused to study the figures from afar then continued into the village. At a bakery she bought a few hard biscuits to eat later and inquired about the statue. Too busy to answer her question, the cashier told her to stop at Le Musée Fantastique de la Bête du Gévaudan just down the street.

At the museum she heard the story of a woman and a beast. In the eighteenth century, as the tale goes, a huge wolf left the forests of nearby Ardeche and came south to the area around Saugues. About the time the wolf was first spotted, a human baby disappeared. Rumors created by this coincidence caused panic across the region, and people began to say the wolf, strangely orange and as big as a small donkey, had killed dozens of women and children. Early in the 1760s, fifty soldiers were sent by Louis XV to slay it, but the animal eluded them. Peasants, simple and devout, believed the beast was either a hellish demon on the loose or divine justice at work as required by God.

She left the museum, ate lunch at a nearby cafe, then returned to the trail pondering the meaning of the statue. During the afternoon she came to a farm with two houses, one of which displayed a "Gite de France" sign, and seeing a barn nearby with a water trough for animals, turned in to fill her bottle with water jetting from a pipe. The farmyard was strangely absent of people, but there was a collection of tables and chairs shaded by umbrellas on the far side of the lawn. Hoping to eat dinner without having to stay the night, she walked over to the patio, chose a table, and sat down to wait. About the time she began to think she was being ignored, a man came out to serve her. Since it was too early for a complete meal, he offered only one item, rabbit with artichokes and onions sautéed in a sauce of white wine, mustard, and cream. She had never eaten rabbit and hardly had ever eaten artichoke, but since it was the only item ready, she accepted the offer. Curiously, when the waiter came out with her order fifteen minutes later, he did not return to the kitchen but climbed on a nearby tractor, started it up, and in a swirl of smoke and noise drove out to an adjacent field and began cutting alfalfa.

As she ate the rabbit and watched her waiter drive his tractor, a pair of young couples stepped out of the gite and came across the lawn. One of the women, broad shouldered and long legged like Clare, lurched on crutches up to a table and dropped awkwardly into a nearby chair. Her companions sat solicitously around her.

"Bonjour, Madame," said one of the men.

"Bonjour, Monsieur."

"How has your walk been?"

"It has been going quite well, but I see yours has not been entirely successful."

"This is our first and last day on the trail," said the other man. "This morning up in the hills my wife fell on a rock and injured her ankle. We called paramedics, and they brought us to a hospital."

"Climbing down out of the hills must have been painful."

"It was," said the injured woman, "but we had assistance from hikers who helped me to the ambulance."

Clare was not surprised that the woman had been helped. Hikers met, spent time together, then drifted apart, perhaps to meet again, perhaps not. But while they came and went as they pleased, fellowship was commonplace. She herself came upon a woman who had just fallen. While she squatted to inquire about the woman's health and look at her bruised elbow, other hikers arrived and asked if she needed assistance. When the woman said that everything was fine, they helped her up, dusted her off, and on her way she went.

"Now, alas, we'll be on the trail without our friends," said the other woman.

By this time Clare had finished dinner and was preparing to leave. Looking at the injured woman, who had propped her foot up on a chair, Clare said, "Perhaps I'll see you again next year on the trail."

"You aren't staying here tonight? The gite isn't full," said the husband.

"No, I plan to camp farther down the trail."

"The weather is good for camping," added the other man. "You should have a nice evening."

Clare said goodbye, went to pay her bill, then headed back toward the trail. On her way down the driveway, she noticed the waiter had gotten off his tractor and was now taking orders from the little group she had just left.

The Healer

At the end of the day, Clare walked into a stand of trees, set up camp, and read Pirsig until dark. The next morning, she ate breakfast a little after dawn, decamped, and started off. During the morning, she came to a high bluff overlooking a prairie and saw a curious building in the far distance that looked like an ugly black toad squatting on the trail. As she approached, the toad slowly transformed, and by the time she got near, it had become a huge fortress-like stone barn with narrow, slotted windows. Assuming the barn was a remnant of a farmstead that had disintegrated over the centuries, she opened her guide for information and was surprised to learn the barn had been turned into a gite.

Walking around the corner, she spotted a large glass door and entered. The site must have been popular, for although the building seemed miles from village or city, it contained a restaurant with a busy staff, as well as laundry and sleeping quarters for hikers. While eating lunch, she discovered the building was still used as a barn. Through a window she saw a farmer on his tractor retrieving a huge wheel of hay from a nearby field and bringing it toward the gite. Moments later, she heard faint rumbling above when he set the wheel in the hayloft. After lunch, she crossed a river, walked past a farm with a barking white dog, and headed into the hills. Two hours later when she looked back on the prairie below, the huge fortress-like barn had returned to its ugly toad form and looked satisfyingly small.

It seemed to her that neither sky nor sun were as intense in France as they were in mid-continent North America. This lack of intensity, she assumed, was due to humid air coming off the Atlantic and the Mediterranean, and it reminded her of the "Gleaners," a tableau by nineteenth century French painter Jean François Millet. She had never seen the original painting, but remembered a copy of it hanging in one of her university classrooms. In it, three farm women dressed in colorful skirts, large bonnets, and wooden shoes, bend to the ground picking up wheat missed by the harvesters. The broad sky behind them, although filled with hues of pink and yellow, was subdued, as though a glum Millet had muted the sky's radiance to reflect how he felt about the day.

Her perception of the sky led her to be neglectful. She had forgotten to put suntan lotion on her legs that morning, and by early afternoon her calves were reddening. At first she ignored the discomfort, but when her legs became sore, she set her pack down and pulled out a tube of sun-tan lotion. With one foot on a rock, she bent over and was about to squeeze lotion into her hand when she heard someone say, "I can heal that for you." Startled, she looked up, expecting to see the beetle-browed bishop or the priest in Chuck Taylors, but instead, she saw two men sitting quietly in the grass nearby. One of them, an Asian, was looking at her thighs and grinning, the other beckoned her to come toward him.

"I can heal that for you," he said pleasantly.

Perhaps wanting to be polite or feeling tired, she disregarded caution and walked over to the men.

"Turn around," said the man comfortingly.

Like a lamb ready to be shorn, she turned mutely around. The healer mumbled words in a language she did not recognize, or perhaps in no language at all, then began gently kneading her flesh, moving his hands up and down the back of her calves and around her thighs. His fingers felt soothing and comforting, but when they moved farther and farther up her legs and slipped under the bottom of her shorts, she became uneasy. When he yelled at the Asian, who was now snickering libidinously, to shut up, she began to think of bolting. Luckily, at that moment, he pulled his hands away, repeated his priestly incantation, and ended by making a sign with the tip of a finger on the back of her legs. On the brink of losing composure, she grabbed the lotion and pack, murmured thank you, and hurried off. The healer said nothing, but she heard his partner yell, "Madame, I can heal your legs, too. Come back."

Agitated by this distasteful encounter, she walked at a sharp pace until coming to a distant village where a panorama of inhabitants calmly going about their daily business induced her to slow down. She crossed the village, greeting a couple of residents on the way, and on the far side came to a bench where she stopped to pull herself together. At a nearby well she put her face under a spout and splashed cold water over her head as though trying to wash away the memory of the healer and his lewd buddy. She wiped her face on her shirt sleeve, shook her head like a dog coming out of a marsh, and sat on the bench.

The proximity of the villagers and the serenity of the moment encouraged her to relax and think about the incident. Perhaps she had over-reacted, but she could not help scolding herself for responding as she had. She should have ignored the healer's invitation in the first place and not been so trusting. She could manage a self-absorbed college kid on a bicycle trip but knew that alone on the trail she couldn't cope with two unpredictable scoundrels. She vowed never to put herself into a situation like that again.

When her confidence returned, she finally put lotion on her sore legs and rummaged in her pack for something to eat. She found a travel-worn apple, shined it on her shirt, and was about to bite into it when a flock of sparrows began chattering in the treetops. Searching the branches for the boisterous birds and happy to hear the ruckus, she imagined sitting in a crowded courtroom hearing arguments in a legal case. She heard long, blustering statements by one lawyer, counterclaims, just as long and blustering, by the other, and muttering among the audience. The judge was not pleased with this situation.

She sat with apple in hand but refrained from eating as though bound by protocol of the court. But tiring of the legal dispute and wanting to get back to the trail, she finally defied the rule forbidding food in the courtroom. She ate the apple and tossed the core into the weeds with a gesture that frightened the squabbling flock and obliged it to reconvene in another location. In the silence that followed, she sat a few minutes more, then shouldered her pack and stepped onto the trail, her spirits now lightened by a dab of suntan lotion, a little food, and a noisy argument in the avian court above.

She started off at a promising gait but did not go far when a new sound made her stop to listen. Quite unlike the chatter of birds, this sound was coming from the other side of a wall. Curious, she set her pack on the ground, peered over the top, and discovered she was hearing the dull, rhythmic thud of a sledgehammer hitting old concrete. Twenty yards beyond the wall three brawny workers were demolishing a very thick concrete roof beam of an old barn, taking it down chunk by chunk. The man on the roof was smashing the beam with a sledgehammer, another was operating a little crane that lowered the chunks to the ground, and a third was throwing them into the rear of a truck.

As she watched these men toil at their heavy tasks, she wondered if there had ever been any thought of demolition when the barn had been built two hundred years ago. It seemed to her that everything constructed in France was made to be permanent, as though the French could not let go of their past. They enshrined heroes, glorified great deeds, visited history again and again, and created monuments intended to last forever. While permanence seemed good, such clinging to tradition and love of the past made change and modernization difficult. The world is constantly changing, she thought. With all this historical baggage and thick cement, France is not light on its feet.

"Do you have some money for a beer? It is quite hot, and a beer would taste good." The voice, soft and mellow, came from her left. She yelped and whirled around. It was the voice of the healer, who was leaning casually against the wall. Before she could recover, he repeated his request, then approached discourteously close, hand out, waiting.

She stared at the hand, then looked up and stammered, "No, I won't give you any money."

He moved even closer, then murmured, "You have pretty brown eyes. You know you could pay me in another way, don't you?"

"No, I cannot do that."

The healer paused for a long moment, looking into her eyes. "Perhaps another time," he replied, then walked off, his shoulder brushing against hers as he passed. She could smell his sweat.

His arrival, unexpected and silent, left her breathless. She stood for a moment, shaking with fear and anger, then feeling her legs weaken, slid down into the weeds along the wall. She pulled her feet up to her hips, dragged the backpack to her feet as though trying to hide behind it, and sat with arms wrapped around legs in a taut ball. Keenly aware that she and the healer were walking in the same direction, she stayed on the ground until he was long out of sight and would have stayed even longer but knew she couldn't sit in the weeds forever. Finally, she stood up, took a few hesitant steps, then mustering courage, began walking with resolve.

At the end of the wall, she was relieved to see an empty trail ahead, but when the burly workers disappeared behind her and the sledgehammer could be heard no more, she imagined the healer jumping out of the bushes or his partner catching her from behind. When coming to a country road, she took the road instead of the trail, thinking it would be safer, but afraid of getting lost in a web of unmarked lanes and paths, turned around and came back.

Returning to the trail at that moment happened to be a lucky choice for she spotted a pair of hikers ahead of her. Seeing an opportunity for security, she yelled, "Bonjour."

The couple stopped, turned, and waited until she caught up.

"Do you mind if I walk with you? A guy has been bothering me, and I don't want to walk alone."

The hikers looked at each other as though wondering if walking with this frantic woman were a dubious choice. Finally, the man said, "Yes, come on. You are welcome to join us."

The couple began walking but moved so fast that Clare had to hurry to keep up, making her think that perhaps they suspected her of being the crazy one. Not knowing where the healer was, she did not like this haste, for if they passed him hidden in the bushes, he would be behind her, and she more vulnerable later on. Nevertheless, she stayed on their heels until coming to a village. When the trail neared the front door of a bar displaying a Gite d'Etape sign, she asked her fleet-footed companions if they would like to stop for a drink. The man glanced at his partner then replied they wouldn't mind a short break. A bartender in tee-shirt and blue jeans greeted them enthusiastically and escorted them out of a back door to a table under a tree on the lawn. Introducing himself as Alexis, the owner of the gite, he took orders and left.

The couple had hardly said a word to Clare while walking, but now, as if to confirm she was a real hiker and not a crackpot, the man remarked in a dubious tone, "I suppose you've been walking for a time."

"Almost a week," she said, and in a manner intended to discourage doubt, asked, "And you?"

"We started in Belgium a couple of months ago," replied the woman. "Our vacation is almost over, so we'll get a bus at Nasbinals and go back to Le Puy to take a train to Brussels. You had trouble with a man on the trail?"

"I didn't have any real trouble, but he was threatening. He wanted me to pay him for healing my sunburned legs."

"How did he heal your legs?"

"He didn't really heal anything. He massaged my legs, mumbled something unintelligible, and made silly signs. After that he thought I owed him something."

"Nasty people walk the trail as well as good people," said the man, now more sympathetic. "Sometimes it's difficult distinguishing one from the other."

"Yes, I am beginning to realize that. This one was interested in more than money."

"I would say he's a predator," said the woman.

"I felt like that woman fighting the wolf in the green sculpture back along the trail."

"The woman and a wolf? Where did we see that statue?" asked the woman.

"It was just before we dropped into Saugues," replied the man. "Remember? We walked across a meadow to look at it up close."

"Yes, yes, I remember now, the wolf soaring through the air, the woman's skirt swirling as she turned to face him, her braids flying, and her stick poised to fend off the beast. The whole scene was spectacularly dynamic."

"That statue," said Clare, "is based on a myth about a large wolf that killed many women and children, some say hundreds, up around Saugues. Peasants in the region at that time believed the beast was a sign of God's anger, and the affair eventually grew into a religious tale."

Returning with the order, Alexis overheard the conversation about the peasants and wolf. He placed the drinks on the table, sat down, and in a loud, jovial voice tinted with an unusual accent, began a different version of the story. "The attacks happened here in this region, not up there in Saugues, and it didn't kill many people although it might have killed one or two." Then he went into a long story about how the animal eluded soldiers for years but was finally killed by a royal hunter.

When Alexis came to the end of his version of the beast story, the Belgians had finished their break and were ready to move on. They thanked Clare for the drinks, wished her good luck, and commended Alexis for his excellent tale. He wished them a pleasant walk and pointed to a gate at the back of the lawn. When they were gone, he picked up the glasses, wiped off the table, and assuming Clare too would soon leave, went back to the bar.

But Clare did not leave. As Alexis was telling his version of the story, she had seen the healer walk past on the trail. She wondered how he had gotten behind her. Since their last encounter, there were no villages or places to stop, only fields, forests, and brush along the way. Uneasy about returning to the trail, she went to the bar and asked Alexis about a bed. When he said one was available, she took it, had a beer at the bar, and left to take a long shower and wash clothes.

While waiting for her clothes to dry on an outdoor line, she grabbed *Zen and the Art of Motorcycle Maintenance*, found a shaded place on the lawn, and started reading. By now she had read enough of Pirsig to discover a similarity between his book and Kerouac's *On the Road*. San Francisco was the narrator's goal in each novel. Kerouac's narrator went to the city searching for his version of Zen, and because of the title of Pirsig's book, she assumed his narrator was also going there for the same reason. She read unhurriedly, pausing occasionally to think about Pirsig's philosophical observations. After an hour of prairie roads and philosophy, she closed the book and went to gather her things from the line.

When she returned to the lawn, the gite had begun to fill with hikers. Some were looking for dormitory beds, a few were sitting at the bar with a drink in hand, and others were resting on the grass with companions. Two young men pushed heavily loaded bicycles through the back gate. On the back of one bike stood a black guitar case attached to the saddle. They leaned their machines against a wall and went to the bar. When they came out to drink their beer on the lawn, Clare went over to chat. One rider worked for the post office and was on vacation. The other had recently quit his job at a pizzeria and hadn't yet started looking for a new one. They had camped for two weeks and now wanted to clean up and sleep in beds. When she said she came from Minnesota, the rider with the guitar talked admiringly about Prince and Dylan and asked if she had ever been to California. When she said she was born and raised in San Francisco, he pummeled her with questions about the California music scene until his riding partner pulled on his shirt sleeve saying it was time to find beds and take a shower before dinner.

While Clare was sitting at the bar after the Belgians left, Alexis told her that the gite was not far from the village church, and he attended evening prayer whenever he could. Wanting to encourage hikers to attend, he had attached a conspicuous notice of vespers to the menu posted near the front door and had invited the local priest to dine with them that evening. When the cleric, indistinguishable from hikers except for his collar, arrived, he chose a table, sat down, and chatted easily with fellow diners.

After dinner, guests moved to the bar or went to sit on the lawn and enjoy the waning day. The priest stopped on his way out to talk with Alexis's mother, the gite's cook, who had finished her work and was playing Scrabble with friends at a picnic table. Little groups formed here and there on the grass, and by chance he sat in the same group as Clare. He had walked segments of the trail, and as the evening passed, told amusing stories of his adventures and misadventures along the way.

Although he was part of the group, a comment by one of the hikers who had gone to vespers pressed him to reply as a priest. The hiker said, "I am not walking to worship at the shrine, but it was uplifting to receive your blessing and encouragement."

The priest responded, "I see encouraging all walkers as part of my job, not only the believers."

"You see no difference among walkers?"

"Of course, I do," said the priest. "Christians are a select group with strong beliefs in God and a long tradition of worship, but we are all part of God's creation."

The priest's comment reminded Clare of the two clerics she had met along the trail. While he lived among the people and encouraged all walkers, the two men on the trail set themselves apart with an irritating superiority disguised in piety. The difference between them and the priest characterized religion in general, she thought. There were the elite, whose preoccupation was power and politics, and the common, who were occupied with food shelters and global charity.

The conversation with the priest ended when a woman on the other side of the lawn shouted, "It's getting late and time to go to bed, but before we say goodnight, I have an Australian Aboriginal good-evening dance to teach you. Stand up, everyone!"

Scattered groans arose from the tired crowd, but not to be denied, the Australian put a tenacious foot inspiringly forward and waited until the willing and acquiescent were on their feet. Ignoring those who remained sitting, she raised her arms in an Aboriginal pose, planted one foot in the grass, and let the other one swing forward. The lesson began. The would-be dancers moved their arms and feet in imitation of their leader, and after mastering a few steps, began making awkward swoops around the lawn. For a few moments, the dance appeared as though it might take form and flourish, but in time the less confident, ignoring the heartening shouts and brave comments by those on the ground, began to pull away and join the unwilling. The dance then fell apart, and the Australian was obliged to bring her simple steps to an end. She heartily praised her dancers for their effort as they turned toward their beds. The priest said goodbye to those around him, stopped to say good evening to Alexis's mother, who had finished her game, then walked through the back gate and disappeared into the night.

As Clare lay in her bed waiting for sleep that evening, she thought about Alexis and the priest. She understood why the blunt, straightforward gite owner liked the cleric. Each man had a pragmatic, benevolent manner about him she admired. She recalled how Alexis had told the story of the Beast of Gévaudan. His matter-of-fact version of the myth had made it nothing more than an interesting historical conflict between humans and nature, and he had told it in the same fashion as the sculptor, who had created the kinetic green statue along the trail. In posing woman against beast, the artist had elevated each adversary to a plain above religion. The woman fought alone, relying solely on her own strength and wit, and the beast represented neither good nor evil. Both beast and woman were creatures of evolution and nature, no more, no less.

Having slept on a bottom bunk, she slid out of her bag, quietly packed, and left the dormitory early the next morning. After breakfast she asked Alexis to sign her créanciale then left, hoping the healer was far down the trail. Later in the morning she came across an intriguing dog. As she walked out of a forest and turned to take a tarred road up a hill, she saw a Saint Bernard lying in the shade of a tree and watching cows eating grass at the edge of the road. Since the cows were outside the pasture, she thought the dog's job was to guard the herd until a farmer arrived. But when she strode onto the pavement and went up the hill, he followed her, loping easily at her side. At first it was pleasant to have a companion, but thinking she had somehow lured him away from his job of tending cows, she began to feel ill at ease. She should not have worried, however, for after a few minutes, he sprinted up the hill and left her behind as well.

She watched the wayward dog disappear over the crest, then followed. At the top of the hill, she saw a large, flowery meadow below, bordered on one side by a stand of trees. She descended to the meadow's edge and began crossing, feeling as though she were stepping into a lake infused with aromas and colors. She did not go far into the lake, however, when hearing the faint but unmistakable call of a cuckoo coming from the nearby woodland. She stopped to listen, her attention shifting from colors and odors to sound and emotion. Unlike the excited dispute among the sparrows in the avian court, the call of the cuckoo was rhythmic, gentle, and soothing, almost sad, and it sent a ripple of poetic nostalgia through her. Imagining it singing to a dying mate or calling lost children, she remembered her grandmother's recordings of Beethoven and Mozart, who imitated the cuckoo's call so well in their symphonies. She recalled hearing her grandmother reading stories about cuckoos and waiting with her for the little bird to pop out of the tall clock in the living room. And she thought about the plantation children in the movie *Out of Africa*, who stood at the door of Karen Blixen's house fascinated by the mechanical cuckoo that announced the hour.

Although romantic by nature, Clare was scientific by training. When she walked farther into the meadow and could no longer hear the call of the cuckoo, her point of view changed from that of poet to that of scientist, and her romantic view of the bird collided with reality. Cuckoos were not quite what Beethoven and Mozart suggested in their lovely melodies. During nesting season pairs of cuckoos search for nests of smaller birds, and when those birds are out foraging, the female cuckoo lays an egg amongst the eggs already there. When the foraging female returns to discover an extra egg in her nest, she breaks and shovels it over the side, determined to rid her nest of the foreigner. But sometimes she mistakenly breaks one of her own. If a cuckoo hatches and there are other eggs or chicks in the nest, its instinct from an early age, even before it can see, is to push them over the side and remain as the only child. Alone, it is fed and pampered by its unknowing hosts, growing massive in the little nest like an indolent, spoiled child, until ready to fly away.

When the conflict between nostalgia of the poet and reality of the scientist receded, she put the cuckoo out of mind and returned to the hues and aromas of the lake. Stopping to examine flowers close to the trail, she saw a small cluster of flowers whose dry petals and gray tints indicated their blooming season had come to an end. But there were other flowers whose form and brilliance showed mid-season energy and life. Nearby were plants with bright white blossoms. When she moved the stems of one to look below, she saw a red and metallic-black stink bug ambling over a leaf on the ground. She imagined that from its point of view, the blossoms above looked like colorful hot air balloons floating across the sky. On the other side of the white flowers, she saw a cluster of round, purple flowers on long stems, and beyond them, flowers she recognized, blue sage and yellow cowslips below, and brooms, sweet and redolent, fluttering above. Since the meadow produced a continuous rotation of flowers all summer long, it was an ideal environment for honeybees.

She looked toward the woodland, pleased to see white wooden hives nestled among the bushes under the trees, then continued crossing the meadow. When reaching the far side, she stopped and turned to admire the flowers. But instead of seeing the colorful lake she had anticipated, she saw a man step into the water on the opposite side and come toward her. Unable to recognize him at that distance, she thought of the Healer, and the calm waters of the colorful lake suddenly swirled into a tempest of fear. Her first reaction was to dive into the flowers, but since they offered no real place to hide, she fought her fear, stayed stubbornly on her feet, and watched the man close the distance. When he reached the middle of the lake, the tempest began to subside, and fear abate, for unlike the healer, this man moved as gracefully as the Saint Bernard. And when he gazed pensively across the meadow, perhaps to admire the flowers as she had done, she knew he was not the healer.

By the time he crossed the meadow, she had regained her composure, and when he came near, she said, “Bonjour, Monsieur.”

In spite of the deliberate calmness with which she addressed him, the man stopped abruptly, startled by an unexpected voice. Seeing his reaction but not knowing quite what to do, Clare blurted out, "May I join you?"

If he had been French, he would have commented loudly on her rude greeting, but instead he peered at her for a long moment, relaxed a little, then replied, "If you like."

"Thank you," she responded.

He resumed walking, and pleased to have found someone to walk with, she fell into the rhythm of his pace at his side. He said nothing as though lost in thought or unsettled by the unexpected way they had met, and after walking a distance, she started to feel uncomfortable and began searching for a topic of conversation. At first she could think of nothing interesting to say but finally decided to start with the Saint Bernard. She began as though speaking to thin air but when describing the dog's fickle behavior, he finally responded.

"Saint Bernards are rescue dogs, originally bred in the Western Alps. I think the one you met was a stray who found cows to watch, and when he saw you, he assumed you needed help."

Thinking back to the incident of the previous day with the healer, she thought the dog rather perceptive and wished he had stayed with her.

She realized the hiker was not at ease using the French language. Wondering if he could speak English, she switched to that language, and he began to speak more freely. The previous year he had walked from Amsterdam to Santiago and on this way back was stopped by severe weather in the Pyrenees. He was now making the trip a second time earlier in the season.

"Why are you taking the trail again?" she asked, somewhat intrusively.

Surprisingly, he responded. "I'm not sure why I began the first time. I think I just wanted to get out of the city and see the countryside. But somewhere along the way I began to like the contemplative aspect of walking. Now I crave the time alone to meditate."

"I suppose there are a lot of things to contemplate," she noted, wryly.

"Of course, there are," he replied earnestly, "as many things as you can imagine, although I often think about nature."

"I wonder if walkers of long ago felt as connected to nature as we do today."

"We don't feel part of nature today," he responded. "We see ourselves as separate and superior, able to control nature with chemicals, construction, and invention. Modern hikers go into nature without really being part of it. Some day we will regret our attitude of superiority."

"To have so much time for walking and thinking, you must have summers off as I do."

Either too shy or too centered on his own thoughts to ask about her, he replied, "I'm a piano teacher. Last year I lent my few summer students to a fellow piano teacher when I took to the trail."

"I suppose private teachers have the same worries and rewards we public teachers have."

"I enjoy teaching motivated students, but not the ones who are taking lessons just because their parents think they should."

"What makes a good pianist?"

It was evident he had thought about that question. With little hesitation he declared, "I can think of a number of attributes that make students good pianists. The better pianists start young. They have good technique, which comes from hours and hours of proper practice, and it is something most students can develop if they work hard enough. They have insight into a composer's style, which comes from analysis and study of compositions. Composers can be identified by their themes and styles. Sometimes they put an unusual note into a pattern, change key, or deform a pattern to surprise and please, and good students are able to discern these patterns and respond to them. Finally, they have enough imagination to interpret artistically what composers have written. Music has rules, but imaginative pianists are not tightly rule bound. Only occasionally do I get a student with all these qualities at a high level, and that student usually leaves for a conservatory."

"That must be frustrating."

"I've learned to accept it. Conservatories have more resources than I do, and they provide degrees and diplomas. Actually, I encourage exceptional students to go on."

"Have any of your students become well known pianists?"

"I've had some who are regionally known as soloists and orchestra members but so far none nationally. Many of my students get involved in other things and never become public pianists, but I think they take advantage of the piano in one way or another. Many are changed by the instrument, and I am sure most will play their entire lives."

"How are they changed?"

"They're changed in many ways, some obvious, some subtle. By studying piano, the world of music opens up to them. They discover the genius of composers, the poets of sound and rhythm, whose music ranges from simple to complex in many styles. They learn to appreciate the work of musicians. I'm not talking just about other pianists, but all types of musicians from classical to popular."

"I suppose you give concerts either as soloist or partner with your students."

"No, I'm not a concertist."

"That's surprising. Why don't you perform in concerts?"

"The primary sensory mode for good pianists is auditory. I'm a visual person. I should have gone into photography or painting. Maybe that's why I like hiking across the country."

Clare thought the piano teacher had relaxed with her at his side, but when the topic of music came to an end, he reverted to his habitual, pensive introversion, making her wonder if her barrage of questions had caused him to reveal more than intended. They walked a little farther in silence until he said, "It's time for me to move on."

Reluctantly, she replied, "Thanks for the pleasant conversation," then unable to think of anything else, added lamely, "It's been illuminating."

"Bonne route," he said as he walked off, reminding her again of the Saint Bernard when it left her and loped over the hill. She thought of saying they might meet again, but as he lengthened his stride and moved away, she refrained, believing that meeting again would never happen. Soon he was far down the trail, once again the solitary aesthete she had seen crossing the meadow, unsuited for concerts but fit for the long trek to Santiago and, she assumed, to the sea.

When the piano teacher was gone, she turned to look across the land, wondering what he saw. The countryside was now changing to a swelling, rolling prairie, veined with creeks spanned by narrow stone-arch bridges. This was the region of Occitan, where villages and cities had granite hard names like Aurillac, Bergerac, d'Olt, Campagnac, and Rignac. She knew of two cities in this region, one by the internet and the other through the theater. While studying weather along the trail in preparation for the trip, she had discovered Aurillac, often the coldest city in France even though it was in the south. And she knew of Bergerac because it was the village from which came Cyrano, a sadly romantic man with an excessively large nose, in the famous play by Edmond Rostand.

Occitan is a land of beautiful cows, she thought. She recalled standing aside in the mountains near Le Puy at the beginning of her walk, watching a farmer pushing his bicycle as he led his herd to pasture. She couldn't forget the last cow in the herd, whose eyes revealed great physical effort. Her rear hip, damaged either by accident or arthritis, rotated awkwardly under thick hide as she limped to keep up. Here, though, farther south and west, cows seemed to be in perfect health. Grazing in fertile, green pastures and drinking from springs and mountain streams, they were sleek and lovely. Some stood on hilltops, silhouetted black against the sky, some grazed on hillsides, and others idled near the trail, placidly chewing their cud as they watched her trudge past.

At the beginning of her walk, she could identify only slender Holsteins and massive Charolais, both common in the Midwest. But along the trail she learned of other breeds. She had seen two breeds that looked like Holsteins although they were not Holsteins because their black and white colors had not been applied so neatly. One of these, the Vosges, which may have come from Scandinavia, looked as though a careless painter had splattered black paint on a white cow creating a messy version of a Holstein. The other, the Pie Noire, looked like a black cow spattered with white paint, as messily applied as the black to the Vosges. She had seen Jerseys, imported after World War Two to replace herds destroyed in battles, and Normands, bespectacled cows from the north with patchy red-brown coats. Occasionally she spotted a horned, brown breed difficult to milk, called Salers, which came from a region north of the trail. And she saw Aubracs, short-horned, light brown cows that originated in the region she was now crossing. She found something serenely soothing in all these passive creatures.

Incident at Decazeville

She kept hiking southwest until coming to a brook where she decided to camp. Wanting to avoid being seen, she followed the stream away from the trail until it took a sharp bend behind a low ridge. A little beyond this bend she came to a narrow beach a few inches above the water, and ignoring the possibility of rain, set up camp on the sand. When everything was in place, she sat next to the gently rippling water and while watching crayfish and minnows move about in the shallows, ate a sandwich, an orange, and some dried figs. After dinner she washed a few items of clothing and laid them on the ridge of the tent hoping they would dry in spite of the damp night air.

After evening chores, she read Pirsig and got far enough into the book to discover it was quite unlike Kerouac's novel. Although she hadn't liked the dissolute, self-indulgent personality of Sal, the narrator in *On the Road*, she thought he was well drawn with hues and shadows that reminded her of the rocks in the foundation of the church photographed by the hiker from Paris. Pirsig's narrator, on the other hand, seemed flat and less complex.

She had walked more than twenty miles that day, and although the terrain was relatively flat, she was weary to the bone. When the sun began to set, she put the book aside and climbed the ridge to scan the landscape. Cows were gone to barn, a single clump of trees stood motionless in the distance, and prairie grass lay silently still. Seeing no humans, she returned to camp, disrobed, and stepped into the stream to bathe herself in the cold water and enveloping darkness. Before going to bed, she pulled the soldier's knife from its backpack pocket and as caution now seem to require, threw it into the tent. She crawled in, slipped into the sleeping bag, and while lying on her back, opened the knife and lay it within reach. In the quiet stillness of the night, hidden from the trail, she soon fell asleep.

During the night she awoke thinking she heard movement near the tent. She slid her hand down to the knife and listened for many minutes, but hearing nothing more, assumed it was an animal of the night and drifted back to sleep. The next morning, she awoke refreshed and energetic, and pleased to meet a new day, slipped out of the tent as the sun was rising. Soon cows would return to their pastures and gentle winds rise to stir the prairie grass. The pleasure of the sunrise was tainted, though, when she discovered that a pair of panties was missing from the tent roof. Thinking of the noise during the night, she looked for tracks, but the narrow beach gave no clear evidence of footprints, animal or human. Perhaps a gust of night air had blown them into the water, and they had floated away.

After breakfast, she decamped, followed the stream back to the trail, and began hiking. During the morning she saw a group of people on a bridge in the distance, and when arriving was pleased to see dirty, all-terrain bicycles leaning haphazardly against boulders near the end of the bridge. The bicyclists were sitting on the bridge's stone railings eating snacks and drinking from their water bottles. Some looked out across the landscape, and others watched Clare as she approached.

Looking up at the travelers, Clare said, "Bonjour."

"Bonjour," said a woman in reply. "We watched you coming along the trail. It looks lonely to be walking by oneself in this big country."

"I'm not entirely alone," said Clare with a smile. "I see cows occasionally."

"You're only the second person we've seen this morning," said another.

"You've seen another hiker?" asked Clare, a bit startled. "Was it a man or woman?"

"It was a man."

"Do you remember what he looked like?"

"We met him a few miles west of here. I didn't pay much attention. All I remember is that he seemed unwashed and shabby. Have you seen him before?"

"I may have met him a couple of times."

"The landscape here is strange, like a treeless, grassy moon with streams of water," noted another biker. "The prairie, gray and green, rolls on and on."

"It's nice to get out of mountains and forests," said Clare, and hearing an unfamiliar accent, she asked, "Where are you from?"

"We're from Andorra."

"Is Andorra part of Spain or France?" Clare asked.

"You must not be from this region either," said another rider. "Where are you from?"

"I'm an American."

"Well, then I suppose you can be excused for knowing so little about Andorra. Andorra is an old, independent principality in the Pyrenees between France and Spain. It's made up of seven parishes, which I suppose you Americans would call states. You should come for a visit someday. You like skiing and mountaineering?"

Charmed by the banter of the Andorrans, Clare responded, "After the Camino I might do that, but I'll have to learn to ski."

"Andorra would be a good place to learn. I'm sure you would like our country," replied a woman.

The conversation about their country had hardly started when the Andorrans' break came to an end. They descended to their bikes, squeezed tires, adjusted loads, and mounted. With one foot on the ground, they looked up at Clare, wished her "Bonne route" and "bonne continuation" and started off toward the northeast. Taking their place at the railing, she watched the riders cross the prairie, their bicycles rising and dipping with the lay of the land. When they were out of sight, she stepped off the bridge and headed in the opposite direction, feeling a little queasy about the hiker ahead of her.

A couple of hours later she walked into a town and passed a building with a sign Workers' Café painted in white letters on the front window. Never having eaten in a workers' café, and curious about the food and clientele, she turned off the sidewalk, climbed a couple of steps and pushed open the door. Inside, she set her pack on the floor and assuming a card or pass was not needed, waited near the entry for a table. The interior was practical and unsophisticated. Unpainted wooden tables were aligned more or less in short rows, and except for a large bar facing the door, the relaxed decor reminded her of small-town Minnesota cafes.

A sign at one end of the bar displayed the menu of the day.

Entrée : Velouté Glacé aux Tomates

Plat : Mignon de Veau Légumes

Dessert: Pommes Farcie au Four

A waitress came and seated her, set a basket of bread and a carafe of water on the table, and took her order. While she waited, Clare studied the patrons around her. Nearby was a table of men deeply involved in a conversation about transportation strikes and pensions. Beyond them were groups of women in dark pants and light blouses. The women looked like office workers, but the men, muscular and broad shouldered, seemed too big and burly for an office. She assumed they were masons, plumbers, and street repairmen. In typical French style, everyone dined gracefully, eating slowly, and enjoying their hour off.

The entrée consisted of a large tomato almost hidden in a mixture of cubed ham, cubed cucumber, onions rings, zest of orange, and parsley. The plat principal was a large filet of veal lying in a bed of carrots, celery, mushrooms, and penne pasta, all lightly covered with a film of butter and a layer of parmesan. As she made her way through the entrée and plat principal, she wondered how the workers could eat so much and thought it had been a mistake to order dessert, but when the apple stuffed with orange zest, dates, and raisins, all covered with cream, arrived, she ate every bit, although resisted licking her plate. She ended lunch an hour later with a small cup of coffee accompanied by a little square of dark chocolate and a packet of sugar the size and form of a half-pencil. After coffee she paid her bill, rolled out the door, and started down the trail, moving a little slower than when arriving.

Crossing the northeastern edge of the Averyon in the Midi-Pyrénées region, the trail brought her to the forested hills above Estaing, where she had to make a Hobson's choice. She could follow the highway, an easier but longer route around the base of the highland, or she could climb into the hills and take the shorter, more difficult trail. She decided to take the trail, not because it was shorter but because it had secluded places to camp. The next morning, she descended to the highway and circled down toward Estaing. She took a bridge over the Lot River but instead of turning left to follow the trail, turned right, and walked into town to have breakfast. From the mountain she had seen a chateau along the river. At that distance, the chateau had the fairytale quality of a Walt Disney castle, but when she entered the town and saw the chateau's rough towers and lichen-covered stone walls up close, the fairytale quality disappeared.

Wandering down a narrow street looking for a cafe, she came upon an unsettling situation. Houses had steep rooftops covered with gray slate. On the roof of one of the houses, she saw a calico cat trying to keep from sliding off and falling to the street three stories below. It had been on the roof a considerable time, she thought, because a small crowd of cat lovers and well-wishers was standing on the street below, hoping for a miracle. While she wondered how the cat had gotten up there, a woman appeared in a nearby open window with a fluffy dust mop. Clare was relieved to think the cat would somehow be pulled through the window into the house and the adventure end happily, but with a swish of the mop, the woman stunned the cat and shivered the crowd by knocking it off the roof. As it fell, frantically clawing air, Clare wondered how anyone could be so cruel to an animal, and when approaching the crowd, expected to see everyone staring at the remains of a cat flattened out at their feet on the cobblestones. Instead, she saw three firemen standing amongst the spectators, holding a blanket, and as she passed, a fourth fireman emerging with the cat under his chin, trying to calm the foolish, unsteady animal.

Clare walked on, found a cafe, and knowing the cat was treasured and safe, ate a tranquil breakfast. When leaving the cafe, she walked past the house from which the cat had fallen, climbed out of the valley, and made her way to the famous medieval city of Conques, a traditional starting point for hikers. When inquiring about a place to stay, she was directed to the Abbaye de Sainte Foy just behind the church. After paying for bed and board in the entry, she was instructed to put her hiking boots on a shelf with dozens of others and her backpack in a fumigated plastic bag along the courtyard wall. She then followed a volunteer up a narrow white stone stairway to the second floor, where he pointed to a bunk in a large dormitory and showed her the shower room.

After washing dirty clothes in the laundry and hanging them on an outdoor line, she took a shower and found a quiet place to read Pirsig. By this time, she had determined his book was not a travel adventure but a book of philosophy quite beyond her knowledge and experience. In spite of this impediment, she continued chipping away at Pirsig's block of metaphysical marble, laboriously trying to expose the form within. She had never studied Eastern or Greek philosophy, or for that matter any philosophy at all, and wondered how he planned to mix Zen, motorcycles, and art.

That evening she ate a lively dinner with twenty-some other hikers. At the end of the meal, diners were treated to a spontaneous concert by a group of gospel singers who were taking the trail as a group. After the concert everyone was invited to the church to receive the pilgrims' blessing. Given in French, Spanish, German and English, the blessing was reassuring and encouraging, but also troubling. In his prayer the priest had prayed for victims of an accident at the end of the trail. She did not understand what he referred to until the next morning when someone at the breakfast table said that people had been killed in a train crash at Santiago. The news of the accident reminded her that she was not going to a mythical place but to a real city with real people.

During the night she discovered it was not easy for some hikers to sleep close to strangers. She had been awakened by the snoring of a man and heard a couple of shh, shhs from another hiker, and in the morning, an angry woman accused the snorer of being selfish because he had kept her awake all night. As the woman grumbled, it became obvious to Clare and others packing their bags that she had little experience in the ways of the trail and was probably just starting her walk. If she were a veteran hiker, she would have been more tolerant.

The mountains around Conques ascend sharply from the back doors of the village. Before starting out that morning, Clare stopped in front of the church and gazed up into the crags. Among the trees she saw the white steeple of a chapel and wondered if the chapel was close to the trail. She walked out of the village, crossed a shallow valley, and started climbing. Forty-five minutes later she heard music and assumed it came from the chapel organ. But when arriving, she discovered a young man sitting in the shade on a weather-beaten chair playing an accordion. She stopped to listen.

"I've heard that piece before," she said naively. "Is that Piaf?"

"No," said the accordionist with a smile. "It's Satie. Have you heard of him?"

"Yes, I have. His music has a haunting beauty to it. That's probably why I thought it was Piaf."

"Sometimes his music is like a conversation between two people," added the accordionist.

When the musician finished that song and the next, she threw a couple of euros into his hat and moved on, feeling a little less heavy footed.

On the plateau she came to a cluster of houses, descended a gentle slope, and passed a luxuriant garden at the bottom. Beyond the garden at the top of the next rise, she saw a covered spring on the left and a very rustic gite of tan and brown stone on the right. Although most hikers who start the day at Conques do not stop here because the distance is too short, she decided to pause for lunch.

Near the door of the gite a stake poked haphazardly up through the weeds. From it dangled a sign with the word donativo, which meant the owner depended on donations rather than on fixed fees. She went to the open door and peered into the dimly lit interior. The ceiling was low, and the stone floor uneven and dirt-lined. To the left was a kitchen with a small refrigerator, stove, and a set of unsteady shelves. The cooking area was lit by two narrow, horizontal windows and a feeble light bulb hanging from an electric wire over the stove. To the right stood a sturdy table with benches upon which patrons sat and talked. She thought that at one time the kitchen had been the stable of a barn.

Sébastien, the tall, lean proprietor, was dressed in worn, black jeans, a new short-sleeve, plaid shirt, and old sandals. He came from behind the stove, introduced himself with a southern accent, and, since the indoor table was full, escorted Clare to a shaded outdoor table where other hikers were sitting on tree stumps waiting to be served. He offered a choice of water, coffee, various teas, and several syrups that mixed with water, then stepped hastily back into the kitchen. He had not taken her order because there was only a single choice for lunch.

Sébastien earnestly desired to please his guests, but he could not do everything on time. Most hikers were patient, and some were helpful. One woman came out of the gite with a container of lettuce, washed it in the covered spring across the trail, and carried it back to the kitchen. But a few were critical. A woman who sat across from Clare complained about the lack of cleanliness and suggested avoiding the outdoor, dry toilet behind the shed on the other side of the trail. In due time he finished preparing a ratatouille of vegetables from his garden and began serving. There were no complaints about lunch.

After lunch Clare stayed to help clean up. Her first task was to get water from the spring and heat it on the stove. When the water was hot, she poured it into two large dishpans and began washing dishes. Sébastien, meanwhile, cleared tables, took out the garbage, then came into the kitchen to dry dishes. As they worked in the semi-darkness, she discovered he was as garrulous as he was deferential. He had picked up his accent while on alternative military service in the south. During summers he cultivated his trail garden using water from the covered spring. When hikers were scarce, he worked at converting his barn into a clean, modern gite, and during winters he worked for a nearby village as gardener, tree trimmer and handyman. Sincere and devout, he had walked to Santiago from Le Puy-en-Velay and seemed to believe every walker was on his way to venerate Saint James as he had done. He offered his patrons the best he could and was building his gite to support the faithful on their long walk.

When dishes were finished, he asked Clare if she would like to tour his domain. As curious about his gite as she was about him, she followed him out of the kitchen door. The word tour was a slight exaggeration because he had only two things to show her. The first was the outdoor stone oven standing on four long legs next to the back wall of the building. Opening its heavy metal door to show her the interior, he explained that he could bake ten typical loaves of bread or five large ones at a time. The purpose of this huge oven was to bake bread for his patrons, but if there were any loaves left over, he distributed them among his neighbors.

After showing her the oven, he invited Clare to see the work he had done upstairs in the gite. Near the back wall of the kitchen was a narrow stairway covered in dust, dirt, and spider webs. At the foot of the stairway, Sébastien asked her to take off her boots. She was a little surprised by this request but after following him to the top of the steps, she understood. The stairs brought her to a well-lit, orderly dormitory with three single beds and two bunks, all fresh and well made. The walls of the dormitory, constructed of the same tan and brown stone, were rough but brushed clean, and the oak floor was waxed and shiny. On one side was the bathroom. The shower stall, made of glass and built in a corner, must have given the bather the impression of standing under a waterfall of a stony mountain crag.

A hiker, gray haired, thin, and as garrulous as Sébastien, arrived just as they were descending the stairs. Having pulled a one-wheeled trailer packed with camping equipment, dog food, and water up the mountain from Conques, the hiker was exhausted, and while he cared for his dog, a gentle, light colored retriever, Sébastien went to the kitchen, found a few leftovers, and brought them out to the picnic table. As the new arrivals began their lunch, Clare thanked Sébastien for the tour, handed him her donation, and asked to have her créanciale signed and stamped. She then left, passing the tilted donativo sign, and returned to the trail.

She walked a short distance up a hill just beyond the gite then stopped to look back. Sébastien was standing below, waving solemnly like a priest blessing his congregation. And when she turned to resume walking, he began singing "Ultreia," the song of the pilgrims, in a clear, tenor voice.

"Every morning we take the trail. Every morning we go farther. Day after day Saint James calls us."

With the song gently resonating in her ears, she climbed to the crest and turned to look back a second time. He was still there, singing and waving, and he continued until she topped the hill and dropped from sight on the other side.

Winding mountain trails gradually turned into wide cow paths, tractor lanes, and narrow tarred roads. Her destination that afternoon was Decazville, which had been famous for hot water spas until coal was discovered in the region, and spas and baths were replaced with pits and mines. During the first part of the twentieth century mules toiled in the tunnels. They became so accustomed to the work that when ten rail cars were loaded, they automatically began pulling them to the entrance. Villagers, pushed by economic conditions, worked as hard as the mules. At one time mine owners proposed buying the town, but the citizens refused. By the 1960s Decazville was known for environmental degradation, high pollution, and vicious strikes. In the 1970s the mines were finally closed when nuclear power replaced coal. Coming to the edge of the valley overlooking the city, Clare saw a huge basin with grassy terraces onto which the city was creeping. Reminded of the hard, rusty mining towns along Lake Superior, she took a tolerant view of the landscape below.

She made her way into the town and stopped at a crowded cafe which had a long, awning-covered patio that edged out onto the sidewalk. She found a table, sat down, and with her back against the outside wall of the cafe, waited for service. As the waiter, moving from table to table, worked his way toward her, she idly scanned the passing crowd. A kid on a scooter moved down the sidewalk on the far side of the street, his progress slowed by pedestrians. On the cafe side, a mother pushing a stroller with a crying baby skirted the edge of the patio, moving at the same slow pace, and on the street an ambulance, siren silent, crawled past, nudging its way through the throng of pedestrians and cars.

The ambulance was beyond the cafe by the time the waiter arrived to take her order. When he returned, he set her drink on the table along with the bill, and she handed him a twenty euro note. He put a ten, a five, and coins on the table then left to tend other customers. She slid the bills under the ashtray and let the coins lie. Just as she was putting her drink to her lips, a gust of wind lifted the ashtray and wafted the bills under the table of patrons sitting along the sidewalk in front of her. She set the drink down, rose from her chair, and squatted near their feet to retrieve the money. But just as she was about to reach for the bills, she looked up and was startled to see the healer coming toward her along the edge of the patio. If she had been thinking clearly at that instant, she would have stayed low behind the table, but instead she sprang up, dropped uneasily back into her chair, and watched him approach.

He was dressed in the same dirty blue jeans and green tee-shirt he had worn the first time they met, and the pilgrim's shell dangled from the side of his backpack. Looking weather-beaten, used, and tired, he was impeded by the same dense crowd that had slowed the kid on the scooter and the mother with the baby, but with firmly set lips and wary eyes he pressed resolutely forward as the ambulance had done moments before.

Seeing the bills still lying on the floor, a man at another table graciously stood up to retrieve them. When he handed them to her, she was partially concealed by his body and hoped the healer, who at that moment was passing directly in front of her, hadn't noticed. She managed a weak smile and took the bills from the amiable patron, hardly having presence of mind to thank him, and the healer moved beyond the end of the patio disappearing into the crowd. She sat immobilized by fear. Where had she passed him on the trail? Had he seen her? Had he noticed her now? She wanted to believe he was no more than a pan handler or a vulgar opportunist living off hikers, but she couldn't stop feeling that she was his prey and wondered to what lengths he would go.

By the time she summoned up enough courage to leave the cafe, a light rain had begun to fall. She put on her poncho, stepped onto the sidewalk, and comforted by the crowd, went with the flow, knowing it would soon dissolve, and she would be walking alone. Thinking more about the healer than where she was going, she took a wrong turn and got lost. Unable to find a GR 65 sign, she faltered at a bridge near the city's edge and stopped to look around, feeling like a weary pup lost and wet.

At that moment, a car came up a side street toward her and stopped across the road. A one-armed man opened the door and stepped out.

"Can I help you?" he asked. "You look lost."

"I think I've gotten off GR 65."

"Yes, you have. Back up the hill about a half mile you should have veered left instead of right."

When Clare wearily said, "Well, I guess I'll have to backtrack," the man proposed an alternate route. "If you cross this bridge, turn left at the other end, and go through a pasture, you'll cross a village and get back on GR 65 without having to turn around. The pasture is wet and muddy, but you shouldn't have any problem if you stay on the path."

"I think I'll take the path. I don't like backtracking."

"How far are you going?"

"I'm walking to Saint-Jean-Pied-de-Port."

"I'm a hiker too. I don't live far from here and have walked parts of the trail before. In fact, I'll be starting another walk tomorrow."

Beginning to get wet, the man retreated to his car, but before closing the door, he said, "Just stay on the path, and you won't get lost."

"Thanks for your help and bonne route tomorrow," Clare replied.

Curiously, she met this man two more times. She spoke to him in the square of his home village later that same day, and again a few days later when he was entering a church as she passed. His lively step told her he was happy to be on the trail.

Hoping that getting lost allowed her to avoid the healer, she crossed the bridge, turned left, and stepped onto a narrow, muddy path. Following the river bottom, overgrown with shoulder high vegetation, and cluttered with fallen tree branches, she came to a village and crossed a bridge that took her back to GR 65 and out into the countryside. Her wet feet and muddy clothes were worth the effort.

Although the rain stopped and the sun began to penetrate thinning clouds, the afternoon was made unpleasant by thoughts of the healer. Unexpectedly meeting the one-armed hiker in his home village uplifted her mood somewhat, and she regained her optimism when coming upon a young woman sitting on a rock, smoking a cigarette. Seeing a backpack on the ground, she pulled up beside her and said, “Bonjour, Madame. You’re hiking?”

“Yes, I am,” replied the woman. “And I see you’re hiking too.”

“I’ve been on the trail a week or so. I’ve lost track of the days. I’m Clare.”

“I’m Natalie. I started just before Conques. I live with my parents in a village near the trail. So, I just walked out the front door and began hiking.”

“That’s quite convenient. Do you mind if I join you?”

“No, I don’t mind. It takes me a while to get used to being alone, and I’m not at that point yet.”

Extinguishing the cigarette under her boot, Natalie picked up her pack, and the two women started off.

"How far are you going?" asked Clare.

"I'm a student at a graphic design school. My course starts in three weeks, so I'll walk a couple of weeks and then come back by train. Are you from the north?"

"No, well, yes. I'm from the north of the United States. I come from Minnesota, which is just under Canada and next to Lake Superior."

"I know where Minnesota is."

"You are a rare French person. Most French know where New York, Florida, Louisiana, and California are. Almost no one has heard of Minnesota."

"Last year I lived in Canada on a work visa. During a vacation, my boyfriend and I rented a camping car, and we drove from Montreal to Vancouver. We camped on the north shore of Lake Superior and then again in Winnipeg. Superior is so big we couldn't see the other side. It's as big as a sea. I liked Montreal with its shops and overhead passageways. I loved camping out in the country. We drove on wide highways that never seemed to turn or end. I remember setting up our tent on the prairie in Saskatchewan. We could see for miles and miles, and at night the sky was full of stars and bright, dancing northern lights. It took us days to reach the Rockies. It must be the biggest country in the world."

The two women chatted throughout the afternoon until arriving at a village where Natalie planned to stay in a chambre d'hôtes that night.

Clare asked, "What is a chamber d'hôtes? I've never been in one."

"It's something like a bed and breakfast in Canada. You have dinner and breakfast with a family at their table and stay the night in a bedroom. They don't have dormitories like gites, and they are a little more intimate. And of course, they cost more than gites."

Descending through an odd mixture of dilapidated houses and expensive, well-tended homes, the two young women came to a two-story house with an orange tile roof and brown shutters. "This is where I stop. I'm not in good walking shape yet and can't go another step."

Clare followed Natalie in to inquire about a bed, but none was available. When she asked about a gite or hotel room in the village, the owner said there was no hotel, and the village's only gite was full for the night. Clare reluctantly said goodbye to Natalie and walked out into the countryside.

The Tour de France

Clare set up her tent, stowed equipment, and after eating a little food, withdrew to read Pirsig. Despite her limited experience in philosophy, she understood that his book centered on a search for a philosophical equilibrium, which he called quality, and that this search depended on a blend of rational and subjective thinking. She read until coming to the limit of her tolerance for philosophy, then closed the book and watched a green worm inch its way across the arc of the canvas until the tent went dark, and she fell asleep.

It was raining lightly when she woke the next morning. She was tempted to stay in her warm sleeping bag but not wanting to be confined to her tent, forced herself to get up. She ate the last of her food, put on rain gear, and crawled out into the weather. Tent stakes were mud-covered, equipment wet, and putting everything in its place without making a mess took time and patience. Back on the trail, she sloshed through puddles of water and slipped on wet clay. Even though her boots were waterproof, her feet got wet when water ran down the sides of her poncho and dripped into them, making her wish she had added a pair of rain pants to her equipment.

Early in the morning the rain stopped and changed to a thick, enveloping fog. In a way the mist was more unpleasant than rain, for she began to imagine the healer suddenly appearing before her out of the haze. She moved at a tentative, apprehensive pace. Coming to a long, low hill, she began climbing but stopped abruptly when seeing the ghostly image of a man ahead of her moving toward the crest. Thinking it might be the healer, she studied the vaguely defined back, wondering what would have happened if he had seen her first in the isolation of the fog. She watched and waited. But when the ghostly figure arrived at the top of the hill, a slight breeze thinned the haze to reveal a man whose bearing was not like the slink and prowl of the healer. This man moved with a vigorous stride that was as reassuring as the ambling, dreamy pace of the piano teacher in the flowery meadow.

She must have thought the mist somehow muted her voice as well as her vision, for she hurried up to the top of the hill and bellowed, "Bonjour, Monsieur," as the man was descending.

She shouldn't have done that. The hiker, an older man, startled out of his thoughts, jolted into the present and whirled around, almost tipping into the mud.

"Excuse me," she said when seeing his alarm. "I should have been more discreet."

The man pulled himself together in a moment, although it seemed like an eternity to Clare, then replied, "Bonjour, Madame," as he peered up at her. "You gave me a shock. The fog made me feel completely alone in this universe."

"May I walk with you, Monsieur?" she pressed on.

In spite of her frightful approach, he did not hesitate, "Yes, of course."

"Thank you," she said, slipping down to where he stood.

The man's affirmative response was a relief, but feeling abashed by her complete lack of etiquette, she introduced herself like a timorous schoolgirl. "My name is Clare. I'm walking the trail."

This would have been an opportune moment for a sarcastic man to reply with a mocking remark. But instead, he said, "Yes, I can see you are walking the trail. Who else would be out in such weather but a dedicated hiker?"

He then turned and continued walking, now with Clare at his side.

"You move a little faster than I," he said. "I suppose your speed as well as your enthusiastic approach is due to youthfulness. You aren't doing some kind of marathon, are you? Speed does not favor enjoying the environment. Though the weather may be disagreeable, one needs to savor the day."

Like an American obsessed with a new exercise routine, she replied, "No. No. When I started, I figured I could do fifteen miles a day and that's what I am holding myself to."

"Fifteen miles a day is pretty fast, but it's not outrageous. You should go at a pace that fits the day, not necessarily at some predetermined speed."

"How do you know what pace fits the day?"

"It's a pace slow enough to be changed by the walk. Arriving at Santiago, one should be a different person. I don't put much stock in bones and saints, but I see walking as a way to reflect on life and eternity. If you haven't changed by the time you reach Santiago, you've hiked too fast, or you haven't been thinking. By your accent I would say you haven't walked far."

Clare was amused by how her slight American accent made natives and hikers assume she was from one place or another in France. But this comment was puzzling. "I got off the train and started at Le Puy."

"That's strange. Why do you have the accent I've been hearing for the last few days?"

"I'm an American," said Clare.

"How does an American pick up an accent from this region?"

Finally, she understood. "My mother's family came from here. She still speaks French at home, so I guess some of her accent rubbed off on me."

"You planning to visit your French family?"

"No. I have no plans to do that. Contact between our French and American families was broken during World War Two, and we have no idea where they live. I assume they live in the Aveyron area, but I don't really know. Where are you from?"

"My name is Martin, by the way. I'm from Geneva."

"How long have you been on the trail?"

"A couple of months."

"I see you are wearing sandals. Aren't they a little fragile for the trail?"

"I had a pair of boots but found I didn't need them and mailed them home along with a few other items. Like many inexperienced hikers I began with too much baggage. The rule of thumb is to carry no more than ten percent of one's body weight."

Martin paused for a moment, as though reflecting on something, and before Clare could reply, added, "In fact, now that I think about it, the ten percent rule should apply to all our belongings. Life would certainly be different with less stuff, much better."

"I suppose then that you are not in the banking business," Clare noted, almost as artlessly as her introduction had been.

"No, I'm not a banker. What gave you the idea I was a banker?"

She blundered on. "You're Swiss. When I think of Switzerland, I imagine cows with bells grazing high in the mountains, a country that avoids wars like a cat landing on its feet, and well-to-do bankers."

"Stereotypes do have an element of truth in them," Martin conceded. "Switzerland has managed to stay out of wars for a long time because it guards the money of countries at war. It's like having two bullies who ask you to hold their jackets while they fight each other. No, I am not a banker, and I don't have any cows with or without bells. I just retired from a career as a city architect, and as soon as I retired, I took to the trail."

"You must have wanted to get out of the city rather badly. I suppose your wife was unhappy to see you leave."

"Actually, she was glad to see me leave. She wanted a vacation before having me under foot full time, and I needed time and space to figure out what to do with the last part my life."

"Have you decided what to do?"

"No, not yet, but I hope to think of something on the way."

During the morning, the mist began to dissipate, and the sun peeked occasionally through the clouds. Clare was pleased to walk with this thoughtful man, and time passed quickly. Farther down the trail they stopped when coming to a small, beige chapel.

"This is a Romanesque chapel," said Martin as he studied its façade.

"How can you tell?"

"You can tell by the simple, symmetrical form of the structure and the semi-circular arch above the door. The Romans used arches in aqueducts, and they brought what they learned about arch technology into the realm of building construction. This chapel is a small, simple building, so you don't see all the elements of Roman architecture. Large Roman cathedrals have pillars, vaults, and towers. The Romans had a great and enduring influence on architecture. The plain and massive Roman style evolved into the lighter Gothic form of the late Middle Ages, which led to the elegant style of the Renaissance. If you stopped at the church in Le Puy or the one in Conques, you would have seen Roman influence up close. Here in Europe, there are many chapels and churches of this kind."

Martin stepped into the chapel, and Clare followed. This time she saw neither troubling shadows nor heard a droning phantom priest as she had in the little church days before. She studied the interior, trying to understand the elements of Roman architecture until her attention was drawn to four large portraits painted on the wall behind the altar. Scrutinizing them from a distance, she asked Martin, "These are remarkable paintings. Who are these men?"

Martin replied, "They are Matthew, Mark, Luke and John, the gospel writers. Some master artist, probably an itinerant, painted them centuries ago."

Approaching the portraits, Clare said, "They seem to be losing their color."

"Yes, disintegration is a chronic problem for art like this, especially in small buildings whose interiors are so exposed to light and weather."

"Will these paintings be preserved?"

"That's a difficult question. France became a secular country early in the twentieth century when church and state officially separated. The government continues to maintain religious monuments, mostly to attract tourists, but it can't maintain them all. I suppose cities and villages turn to private foundations, the Vatican, or UNESCO for help. But there are monuments and works of art all over France, and whoever pays for maintenance and restoration must be selective. I assume whoever owns this church doesn't have enough funds to preserve these portraits properly, so they will probably continue fading away."

With a final inspection of the interior and a last look at the four fading writers, Martin and Clare stepped out into the light of day. They began walking but went only a few paces when she turned to look back at the chapel and ask another, rather simple question, "Do you suppose the writers actually looked like that?"

"No, of course not. These men look like white Europeans. I think the genuine writers looked more mid-Eastern. The painter of these portraits probably had images of his white European friends in mind when he painted them."

A couple of hours beyond the chapel Martin and Clare came to the outskirts of Saint-Jean-Mirabel. Just before turning to take a road into the village, they walked past a memorial standing on a nicely trimmed lawn in front of a building that looked like an elementary school. This memorial, an oversized replica of a racing bicycle standing on a big boulder, was quite different from all other shrines Clare had seen on the trail. A tribute to neither saint nor nobleman, it was more interesting and inspiring to her than any church, chapel, or statue.

She could not resist wondering about the significance of this odd display and asked Martin if he wanted to stop. Unfortunately, he was not interested in crude bicycle racing memorials and said he would keep going. After a skeptical glance in the direction of the bicycle, he wished her good luck and crossed the road. When he got to the other side, he stopped to look back and wave as though forgiving her for the rash introduction, then turned toward the village and walked away. She studied his back and gait as she had on the misty hill earlier in the day, this time though not fearfully but wistfully.

She leaned her pack against a low wall at the edge of the lawn and sat down to take a pebble out of her boot. After putting her boot back on, she stepped up on the wall onto the lawn and approached the strange machine. Its faded red frame was made of long wooden dowels, its tires and handlebar of desiccated black plastic tubes, its spokes of rusty steel rods. She couldn't decide if this monument was a piece of folk art at its best or at its worst, but whether good or bad, she adored it.

A wooden plaque hung from the handlebar. On July 15, 2004, the Tour de France went through Mirabel on its way to Figeac, and the winner of this segment was David Moncoutie, a Cofidis Team rider from northern France. Standing with hands on hips, she read the plaque, stirred by an image of Moncoutie flying victoriously across the finish line with arms raised and crowd cheering. The passion and intensity of Moncoutie's victory reminded Clare of Terry Fox and the imaginary woman fighting the wolf.

She stepped back from the boulder and paused to think about the churches, shrines, and statues she had seen along the trail. The pomp and sacred mythology they represented contrasted sharply with the bicycle's spontaneous, exuberant, folk-art style, and this contrast caused a feather of giddy sarcasm to tickle the back of her neck. She raised her arms high, as Moncoutie had done at the moment of victory, and with a resolute voice that mocked shrine and ritual, proclaimed loudly, "From now on this bicycle will be called The Monument of Moncoutie." She then bowed three times, turned away, and walked back across the lawn. Amused by the idea of the faithful bowing to an imitation bicycle on a big boulder, she stepped off the lawn onto the sidewalk.

She picked up her gear and began crossing the road, but took only a step or two when startled by a cluster of men and women on bicycles sprinting in tight formation around a curve toward her. Pulling back, she watched them approach. The riders were not young, but all rode expensively sophisticated racing machines. Dressed in colorful jerseys, racing helmets, and tight black shorts, they sprinted by so quickly that Clare had little time to distinguish one rider from another. Intent on maintaining speed and formation, no one spoke, and all Clare heard was the whir of spinning wheels. This was the final sprint to the finish line, and like a Tour de France peloton, riders were at full throttle.

Admiring their racing form and wondering who they were, she watched the cyclists fly past and funnel into the village. She then stepped to the edge of the road a second time, cautiously looked both ways before crossing, and was surprised again. A lone cyclist was plodding around the curve toward her. Dressed in the same kind of uniform and riding a racing machine, he was obviously part of the group. Wondering why he lagged behind, she paused to watch.

When he came to the low wall where she had been sitting a few minutes earlier, he stopped, dismounted, and took off his helmet. Having noticed her as he rounded the curve, he said amusingly, "You're the only spectator we've had today," as though he were a professional racer disappointed at the small turnout, "but I suppose one spectator is better than none."

"It certainly wasn't the weather that limited the crowd," said Clare in a matching tone as she looked up into the now clear sky. "Perhaps publicity posters gave the wrong date of the ride."

"Ah, that must have been the problem," the rider replied. "I see you were admiring Moncoutie's bicycle."

"Yes, I was just thinking about his race. It was startling to look up and see a group of cyclists racing toward me at that very moment, a strange sensation."

"I was standing on this little wall when the racers went by in 2004. One of them went down right in front of me. Unlike me he was going too fast around the curve and ended up on the sidewalk. But he got up and kept going. Moncoutie wasn't in the lead at this point, but between here and the finish line down in Figeac he moved up to the front and passed the leaders at the very last instant."

"I see you are a racer."

"I race for pleasure and health with my friends, but that's all. Do you know of Robert Marchand?"

"No, I haven't heard of him. Who is he?"

"On his hundredth birthday he cycled a hundred kilometers. He did a little less on his hundred and fifth birthday. I don't expect to arrive at that age, but I would like to keep in good shape until I die. Do you ride a bicycle?"

"Yes, I do," said Clare. "I put on a thousand miles or so each year, not as a racer but as a tourist."

"Then you know how irritating a flat tire can be. Have you ever watched the French tour?"

"I've watched segments on television but never in person."

"I hope you get the chance to watch an actual race. You'd enjoy it. But don't stand along a road. On flat, straight roads they go by so fast you can't recognize anyone. A good spot for watching is near a sharp curve or steep climb where they slow down. Better yet, be at the finish line above the crowd."

While Clare and the cyclist talked, he began a procedure that she had completed many times herself. He pulled tools and a spare inner tube from the bag under the back of the saddle, turned the bicycle over to rest it on top of the wall, and began fixing a flat. He loosened the back brake, turned the lever that held the axle in place, and pulled the wheel off.

"It's as big as the Super Bowl in the United States," he noted. "Millions of people stand along the road and watch. Millions more watch it on television."

Clare set her pack on the ground, sat on the wall, and asked, "Up close, what's the tour like?"

At first the cyclist, intent on his work, said nothing. Inserting tire irons and sliding them around the interior of the rim, he detached one side of the tire and pulled out the ruined tube. As he inspected the inside of the tire with his fingers, he began describing the racers. "Tour riders have to be in incredible physical condition to race almost 2000 miles in three weeks. Their heart rates drop to thirty beats per minute when resting and climb to 200 or more when competing at their utmost. They average close to thirty miles per hour, so it doesn't take them much time to cover a lot of territory."

He paused to insert the new tube, put the tire back on the rim, and continued. "Most people think the fastest rider wins the tour, but the race is not won simply by the physical force and effort of one person. It's a sport of teams and strategies. There are three types of riders: rollers, climbers, and sprinters. Rollers are the fastest over long distances, climbers are strongest in the mountains, and sprinters are best in short distances. Not many riders, including team leaders, are good at all three."

The cyclist's attention to detail reminded Clare of the old man who had taught her beekeeping, and it was obvious he loved biking as much as the beekeeper loved his bugs. After checking to see that the new tube was not pinched between rim and tire, he attached a small, compressed air cylinder to a nozzle, then pushed the nozzle onto the valve of the tube. Air flowed with a gentle swish and the tire inflated.

"Each team," he continued, "uses all three types of riders to develop strategies that enhance its leader's abilities and make up for his deficiencies. It's impossible to win a race without the work of team members. Teams that have well-trained, careful riders and a measure of good luck will be the most successful. Moncoutie was a climber, so he had an advantage in the hills and mountains around here. The day he won, he helped keep his leader's time low, accumulated points for his team, and earned big money for himself."

As the cyclist put the wheel back on his machine, Clare asked, "Did you ever think about being a tour rider?"

"I wasn't fast enough and didn't have enough time to train, but I would like to have tried. Maybe I could have done it."

He replaced the wheel, tightened the axle lever holding the wheel in place, then turned the bicycle upright and set it on the ground. Lifting the back of the bicycle, he spun the wheel to make sure it was properly aligned, and when satisfied, set the wheel on the ground, and began tucking equipment back into the saddlebag.

"My mates are in the bar drinking beer and have probably forgotten me, but I suppose my wife is wondering where I am. She was ahead of me as usual and probably didn't know I dropped back until she got to the bar."

Putting on his helmet, he mounted the machine and snapped his right shoe into the pedal clip. "Hope you don't have any flats," he said.

"Flats most likely will not be a problem," chuckled Clare, as he started off.

Seeing the riders fly by and being inundated with so much detail about racing, she felt as though she had seen an actual segment of the tour. Instead of admiring gardens and looking at dogs as she often did when entering a village, she thought about the tour races she had seen on television and imagined the summer day in 2004 when riders swept up the road and flew through Mirabel intent on the finish line in Figeac.

Warning signs have been put up along the tour route. Roads have been inspected for hazards. sand swept away and cracks filled. Throughout the morning thousands of spectators pull in along the route, parking their cars and RVs wherever they can. While the spectators wait, advertising cars flow past, their occupants throwing sample products or cardboard imitations of their products into the crowd. Photographers on the backs of chauffeured motorcycles follow, looking for spectacular shots. And finally, television helicopters fly over, taking videos of landscapes, castles, and crowds. Enthusiasm mounts with the passing of each car, motorcycle, and helicopter, and erupts when riders finally appear. At steep climbs and sharp turns, spectators edge out onto the road to get close to their favorite rider, creating an impression that competitors are riding into a snow squall. Sometimes spectators, youthful and audacious, step out of the crowd and run alongside cyclists, pushing them up an incline or yelling in their ear to do their best. Racers are moving so fast that runners stay abreast only a few seconds then must move quickly aside or risk getting hit by a rider from behind. At moments like this, lives of racers intertwine with those of civilians, and because the crowd is so close to the contestants, foolish things happen.

The bicycles of the racers were arranged in front of a bar when Clare arrived. She was tempted to enter and mingle with the competitors but did not want to get involved in beer drinking at that time of day. She passed the bar, picked up a few things at a grocery store, and started off for Figeac. The trail beyond Mirabel paralleled the race route a couple of miles then intersected with it. When arriving at this intersection, she stopped to look for a GR 65 sign but found none. Through the trees along the highway, she could see a distant city below and assumed it was Figeac but unsure about how to get there, pulled out her "Miam Miam Dodo."

An old man watering his apple trees nearby noticed her thumbing through the guide and shuffled over to see if she needed help.

"Bonjour, Madame," he said in a gravelly voice. "Can I help you?"

"Bonjour, Monsieur. Yes, I think I want to go to that city in the valley."

"You looking for Figeac?"

"Yes, I am, but I can't find any trail sign."

Slipping back to the time of his youth, the man pointed to a house on the far side of his little orchard and said, "I grew up in that house. After high school I got a job as railway ticket agent and left. When I retired, I came back." Pointing to a narrow path that descended from the edge of the road, he said, "When I was a kid, me and my buddies took this path into town. We'd watch movies, smoke cigarettes, and play flippers in bars. You could take that path, or you could keep following the highway. The highway makes a big curve down the hill and will eventually take you to where you want to go, but there's traffic now and then, and it's a lot farther."

"I think I'll take the path. Thank you."

"If you plan to eat lunch in Figeac, I suggest you go to the big terrace in the town square."

The path, well-used and straight but steep, was probably GR 65, although there were no signs indicating so. Clare had no trouble descending. She ran into difficulty at the bottom, however, when the path came to the highway. She turned right, stepped onto the shoulder, and began walking. But when she came to a bridge, her walking space was reduced to inches, and she realized there wasn't enough room for her and the semi-trailer trucks crossing at the same time. Accustomed to tranquil mountains and prairies, she became disconcerted by the din and swirl of traffic and in a panic turned around. Back at the point where she came off the trail, she scurried across the highway, hailed a farmer coming up a country road on his tractor, and asked him how to get into the city. He pointed out a back way.

She crossed railway tracks near a train station, entered the city through neighborhoods, and came to the town square where she found the terrace recommended by the old man. Three shiny black, highly chromed Harley Davidsons were parked along the curb. When she entered the terrace, their owners, dressed in motorcycle jean jackets and boots, were sitting at a table drinking beer. Imagining the unique sound of Harleys, she remembered fondly the gruff, bearded, beer-bellied riders from South Dakota who had stopped to help her fix a flat. Despite efforts to project a tough cyclist image, the riders on the terrace were not American, for even in their biker outfits, they were too refined and slender. She walked past, picked a table, and sat down.

The terrace was shared by the restaurants surrounding it. Waiters hurried back and forth across the streets, dodging cars, pedestrians, and cyclists, to carry full trays in one direction and empty ones in the other. When a waiter arrived and handed her a menu, she asked for something regional. He smiled and suggested that stockfish, the plate of the day, would be perfect. When she asked about the dish, he expounded on the special as though it were his favorite subject.

"It's a fish dish made with zucchini, potatoes, tomatoes, red peppers, and various spices. People have been eating it since the late Middle Ages. Traders bought dried cod on the island of Lofoten, Norway, shipped it south, and sold it in large bundles to merchants on the Mediterranean and Atlantic coasts. Bundles were brought inland on the Tarn and Lot, rehydrated in the rivers, then sold to local buyers. This a very tasty meal."

Trusting this well-practiced speech was not overblown advertising, Clare decided to try the fish.

"You'll enjoy it," said the waiter, who then turned, made his way out among the many tables, crossed the street, and disappeared into a restaurant.

"You'll like the stockfish," affirmed a middle-aged woman sitting nearby. "I have it often. You don't need to be a hungry hiker to enjoy it."

"I'm pleased to hear that recommendation," said Clare. "I hope it's not like lutefisk where I come from."

"What's lutefisk?"

"It's dried cod soaked alternately in water and lye for a week or two. I suppose it also comes from Lofoten. You boil it, then eat it with lots of white sauce or butter. The taste isn't bad, but the gelatinous texture is disgusting. Now only old Scandinavians where I come from eat it. I don't think modern Scandinavians would touch it."

"Stockfish is better, I'm sure. What's your destination today?"

"I'm going a few miles beyond Figeac to camp out in the country. Do you live here in the city?"

"Yes, I do. I'm an administrative nurse at the local hospital. I suggest you take a tour of our city before you leave."

"Back in Mirabel I read that Figeac was a stop on the Tour de France. It must have been exciting to see all those racers in town."

"Oh, no, on the contrary. The race is always a big headache for hospitals. Here in Figeac the population almost doubled the day of the race, operating rooms were set aside, and doctors and nurses were on call."

"Did you treat any injuries?"

"Of course. A photographer on a motorcycle and his driver hit a curb, landed on the sidewalk, and flattened a pedestrian. All three were taken to the hospital. The stupid driver wasn't paying attention."

"Were any cyclists injured that day?"

"If you came from Mirabel, you probably walked part of the course. Riders came out of the hills, descended the highway, and rounded the curve to cross the river. One racer hit a stray dog between Mirabel and here and went down. Luckily, he didn't take anyone with him. When he discovered his bike was wrecked, he threw it at the dog and yelled for a replacement. He would have thrown it at the owner of the dog if he had known who that person was. Another rider hit a poster held by a woman, and he went down taking team members with him. I don't think she realized how fast these racers go."

"What happened to the woman?"

"I don't know. She disappeared into the crowd."

"How about the team riders? Were any injured?"

"They may have been, but we didn't get any. If injuries to racers are minor, they're treated by team medics. It's not unusual to see blood, pieces of fabric, and bicycle parts scattered across the road after big crashes."

"The tour must bring a lot of money into the city."

"It's good for restaurants and hotels but not for the hospital. Our costs are paid by taxpayers since it's a public institution, and even if there are no injuries, preparing for the tour takes a lot of extra work."

As this point in her instructive complaint, the administrative nurse looked at her watch. She put her napkin on the table, took a last sip of coffee, and said, "I must get back to work. Enjoy your stay in Figeac." Picking up her purse and sunglasses, she added, "I suggest stopping at the Musée Champollion. It's not far from here."

Clare watched the woman make her way to the edge of the patio and step into traffic. Since her order had not yet arrived, she pulled out her "Miam Miam Dodo" to see if there was any information about the museum. While thumbing through the guide, she noticed a group of hikers arrive and sit a couple of tables away. When she saw one of the boys in the group wearing a Minnesota Vikings tee shirt, she went over to them and introduced herself as a fellow Minnesotan. The look of bewilderment among those at the table told her that English was not their language, so she switched to French and began again. In that language she learned that a friend of the boy had been at a language camp in northern Minnesota and returned with the tee shirt for him.

The group consisted of father, mother, an older son with two teenage friends, and a five-year-old boy, who at that moment was running around the terrace, climbing on chairs, and talking to people. They had already walked ten miles that day and had more to go. The parents were tired, the teenage boys calm, and only the boy ran around. When Clare asked why the young one was so lively, the mother said that he was being transported in a three-wheeled buggy pushed in turn by the boys. No wonder the teenagers were calm, and the child had so much energy.

Except for a little bag of figs and a nectarine purchased at Mirabel, Clare had not eaten since breaking camp that morning. When the waiter arrived, she said goodbye to the family, hurried back to her table and dug in. Even without being hungry, she would have found stockfish delightful, nothing like lutefisk. After lunch she paid her bill, thanked the waiter for his good advice, and asked how to get to the Musée Champollion.

The Musée Champollion exhibits the work of Jean-François Champollion, an Egyptologist born in Figeac and famous for deciphering hieroglyphics in the pyramids. She toured the museum, then left to explore the town, stopping at interesting little shops as she had done on her arrival in Le Puy. One shop that caught her attention displayed an array of unusual knives in the front window. Entering the shop, she saw an artisan at the back working under a lamp. He was crafting knives designed like airplane propellers. When she asked why he made them in that form, he replied that the city had had an airplane propeller factory since the time of the Wright Brothers. Pointing to a model of a biplane on a high, dusty shelf behind him, he said propeller-shaped knives appealed to tourists fascinated by the romanticism of old airplanes.

Having come into Figeac by the back way, she stepped out of the knife shop wondering where to find the trail. Knowing it often passed near churches, she looked for a steeple rising above the city, and headed toward it, searching for GR 65 on the way. Near the church she found the trail. But just before starting out, she saw the couple coming from the east, whom she had met earlier with the injured hiker.

"Bonjour," she said, and they waved in acknowledgement. "How's your friend doing?"

"She's a little depressed but otherwise okay," said the wife. "She and her husband went home, but they plan to walk again next year."

"How's her foot. Is the injury bad?"

"It is," replied the husband. "Some of her ligaments were stretched, so the doctors had to put her foot in a cast. It's good they did that because she wouldn't have had enough patience to stay off her feet until it healed properly. It's going to take at least three months."

"Are you planning to walk farther today?"

"No. We're going to explore the city and stay in a hotel not far from here."

"Since you're staying in town, I would suggest eating in the central square near the Musée Champollion. Order stockfish."

"What's stockfish?" asked the husband.

"Look for a tall, young waiter in a red shirt, and you will find out when you order it," said Clare. She then wished them good luck, said goodbye, and started down the trail.

A few miles beyond Figeac she stopped to look at her "Miam Miam Dodo." Wanting to orient herself within the region, she determined she was a couple of hundred miles east of the Atlantic and less than that north of the Mediterranean. Turning to scan the surrounding peaks and hills, she thought the region was ideal for raising honeybees. Despite being close to the stabilizing influence of the Atlantic and Mediterranean, the altitude created a climate of temperature extremes well suited for honey production. The penetrating cold of winters required hives to work hard during summers, and there was no time to be indolent as they might have been in more temperate climates. She examined flowers along the trail, anticipating seeing many bees at work, but when finding only a few, she pushed top clusters aside to look beneath. Seeing only a few there as well, she assumed that hives in France were affected by colony collapse syndrome as they were in the United States. Regardless of their small number, it felt good to see the lemon-colored, irascible Italians and the black, gentle Carniolans moving easily from flower to flower intent on their work. She watched and wondered how her hives in Minnesota were doing.

During the afternoon she stopped at a café for coffee. Sitting at an outdoor table, she watched a hefty young woman with a backpack come up the trail. When the hiker arrived, she sat at a nearby table and ordered a Coke. While the waitress was fetching her order, she took a big chunk of cheese out of her pack and pulled a jackknife from her pocket. When the waitress returned and saw the cheese, she wagged her finger at the hiker and said, "Buy lunch or leave." Either not comprehending the demand or put off by it, the hiker said nothing and stared at the waitress. Watching this standoff, Clare thought that perhaps the hiker had no money and offered to buy her something to eat. When there was no response, Clare repeated her offer in English, and the hiker finally muttered, "No, thanks. I'll just drink my Coke and move on." Clare relayed that reply in French to the waitress, who left but kept a suspicious eye on the would-be cheese-eater while tending other customers.

The young woman sat quietly for a few moments, drinking the soda and looking forlornly at the cheese sitting on its oily sack. Finally, she turned toward Clare and asked, "Are you American?"

"Yes, I am. My name's Clare."

"I'm Emma. You going east or west?"

"West. Where you from?"

"San Francisco."

"That's a coincidence. I'm originally from San Francisco. Now I live in Minnesota, where I teach high school."

"I'm a college student."

"Is this your first hike?"

"No, no. I've done places. Last year I hiked in northern Thailand, and I've been in Australia. How about you?"

"This is my first."

Chatting with a fellow American, who had just offered help, encouraged Emma to relax. "It's easy to fall under the romantic spell of France, don't you think?"

"Yes, it is. I like the mountains and pastures and especially the cows."

Looking as though she thought Clare had just left the farm for the first time, she said, "I mean the guys."

"Oh, the guys. The guys here are like those anywhere in the world, I suppose. Some are thoughtful and pleasant, some are unappealingly macho."

"I met two guys touring on bicycles. They were quite charming and not at all macho. They walked with me until one got tired of pushing his bike and left. The other guy, the handsome one, stayed with me. I don't have a tent, so I rented a room in a gite. He stayed in his tent and found me again the next day. He had a guitar and sang to me. Finally, one night he asked me to stay with him in his tent. Well, one night led to another and another."

"So, you don't need to understand French to make love with a Frenchman?"

"I don't understand French when I'm being attacked by nasty waitresses, but I do well enough when talking to handsome French guys."

"What happened? Where is he now?"

"He kept asking about San Francisco, and he said he wanted to marry me. This was a little too fast. Finally, I asked him to go find his partner while I thought about it. After a big cry, he left and here I am walking by myself again, waiting for him to call. Sometimes I think he loves me. Sometimes I think he just wants to find a way to California. When I get back to San Francisco, I'm going to forget about him. Or maybe I'll call him."

"I met him at a gite a few days back."

"You saw him!"

"Yes, I did."

"How was he?"

"I thought he was nice. He's good looking. I wish he would have played his guitar for me."

"You would have liked his music. It's sort of French folk. Did he talk about me?"

"No, I'm sorry, he didn't, but he did ask about San Francisco. He was especially interested in the music scene."

"Maybe I won't call him."

Finishing her drink, Emma grabbed the cheese, put it back into her pack, and said, "Anyway, thanks for the help. Hope they'll let me use the bathroom. I hate squatting in the weeds along the trail. I always feel someone is watching."

When she came out of the bathroom a few minutes later, Emma went to the counter to pay for her drink and left without looking back. Feeling the sting of her disappointment, Clare watched her walk forlornly away.

Emma reminded Clare of another young woman with whom she had walked a short distance. This woman seemed quite the opposite of Emma. She traveled lightly and had a virtuous, unwavering ascetic air about her. "I've been walking more than a month," she said when Clare caught up to her. "I'm a shop assistant in Vienna. I accumulated enough vacation to walk to Santiago and worship at the shrine."

"You've come a long way in a short time," said Clare.

"Yes, I am almost halfway there. I'll arrive just a few days before having to return to my job."

Clare asked the Austrian about life in her country and was curious about her commitment to Saint James, but they hadn't gone far when the hiker abruptly sat on a tree stump and pulled out a fruit bar. When she looked wordlessly off into the distance, Clare knew the conversation had come to an end, and it was time to move on. "Bonne route," she said. "It was a pleasure walking with you," and left.

Oddly, Clare found a similarity between Emma and the Austrian. Even though Emma was worldly and the Austrian religious, both were dedicated to pursuits of imagination, Emma to love and adventure, the Austrian to devotion and sacrifice. And despite their differences, the two women together reminded Clare of her great grandmother Adele. The Austrian was going to Santiago, a great durable oak of virtue, tradition, and safety, searching for religious fulfillment at the shrine, whereas Adele, romantic like Emma, went to San Francisco, seeing it as a blossoming rose bush of opportunity, among which thorns worth the risk of adventure might be hidden.

The Romans

Her tired legs and the setting sun told her it was time to stop for the night. In a pasture near the trail, she saw a shepherd's hut that looked like a tall, peaked igloo built of field stone cemented together by time and gravity. She walked out to the hut, ducked through the doorway, and scanned the darkening interior. Spider webs hung here and there, beer cans and food wrappers lay strewn about, and the dry, dirt floor looked as hard as rock. Since the roof was solid and the door faced away from the trail, she thought this would be a good place to stay for the night. Kicking cans and food wrappers out the door, she unpacked her gear and rolled out her mattress and sleeping bag across the floor. On top of them she dropped her pillow and knife.

Retrieving a sandwich and an apple from her pack, she went outside and sat with her back against the hut. She ate unhurriedly, enjoying the nightfall, and from time to time looked into the sky, waiting for the celestial inhabitants of the night to arrive. The immensity of the heavens reminded her of a crisp autumn morning during her first year of teaching in western Minnesota. As she stepped out of the house to go to school that morning, she glanced across gray, dry bean fields and was startled by a gigantic red sun balancing lightly on the horizon. It was so bright that every object it illuminated tinted red and so fiery that a tidal wave of heat seemed imminent. Its prodigious presence reminded her she was part of an infinitely large and eternal universe.

Sitting in the silent pasture near the path of the first walkers and peering into a slowly illuminating sky, she imagined an endless choreography of stars and planets. She knew that movement of every celestial body was predictable just as the sun's arrival had been that autumn morning before school, and that this celestial movement was subject to Newton's laws of motion and gravity. But she did not have Newton in mind at that moment. Instead, she was thinking about Copernicus, a fifteenth-century Pole, and Galileo, a sixteenth-century Italian, two astronomers who in opposition to church doctrine had proposed that the Earth revolved around the sun. Unlike the first walkers, who adored the setting sun without constraint, Copernicus and Galileo struggled against a coercive religion that stifled inspiration and reason. She considered these two men instrumental shapers of human knowledge, and supreme seekers of truth.

The next morning began warm and clear. Wanting to get an early start, she pulled herself out of the sleeping bag, dressed hastily and packed her equipment. She walked across the pasture to the trail and with a little sack of dried fruit in hand, started for Gréalou. The dry, intensifying heat of the morning reminded her of stories her mother had recounted about how poor the people of this region had once been. Indications of their difficult past were still evident. A gardener was running his rototiller through a plot of ground that looked more like a gravel driveway than a garden. Desiccated white moss covered the tops of stone fences, and pastures, cropped short by sheep and cattle, exposed flat slabs of white rock that looked like toppled, rough tombstones flung here and there by the random hand of nature.

But while a weariness seemed to caress the land, she noticed signs of life and vigor. Hillside vineyards were maturing rapidly, and wild plums, raspberries, blueberries, and apples were ripening along the trail. With the increasing heat of the day, cicadas began a buzz that sounded like pumpkin seeds rattling in dried gourds. It was as though they were being led by a chef d'orchestre standing with baton in hand on a large rock in amongst the trees. When she passed, those nearest the trail lost their focus and the music fragmented, but as she moved away, they re-established their rhythm, the music returned to full vigor, and the concert went on as though she never existed. The dry, metallic but persistent sound encouraged a vague sense of optimism.

About mid-morning she came to Gréalou. Remembering what her mother had said about the village and her family, Clare felt as though she were returning to her hometown after years of absence. Walking down a pleasant, tree lined street into the village, she saw an old couple taking groceries from the trunk of their car and carrying them laboriously into a house. He was tall, white-haired and slightly stooped, she, upright and plump. When the man saw Clare approach with sticks in hand and pack on her back, he smiled and said, "I see we have a hiker. Would you like to come in for a cup of coffee?"

"Yes, yes, I would be pleased to do that," she replied.

The man picked up the last bag of groceries, closed the trunk door, and turning to her said, "Follow me."

The house, constructed of stone and brick, was small and solidly built. The interior, neat and clean, was as hard and geometric as the exterior. Floors were covered with ceramic tiles, cupboards were constructed of dark oak, and the table at which Clare was invited to sit was thick-legged and sturdy. The old man put the groceries on the kitchen counter and sat opposite her, while his wife placed a filter in the coffee maker, threw in a few spoons of coffee, and added water.

"So, you are on your way to Compostelle?" said the old man in a tone of voice that turned an affirmation into a question.

"Yes, I am," she said. "I won't complete my walk this summer, but I hope to finish next year."

"Where are you from?"

"I'm from the United States."

"Ah, yes. We would like to go to America some day, but it may be too late."

"We had family there, but we don't know if they still exist," added his wife.

"I had an aunt, born on a farm near here, who went to America when she was about your age. I didn't know her, but I knew her daughter, who stayed behind with my family for a time," said the old man.

"Why did she go to America?" asked Clare.

"That's a very long story," said the wife discouragingly, as though she did not want a stranger to hear family secrets.

"Yes, it is," replied the husband, ignoring the tone of his wife's voice. Then he began. "When my aunt finished high school here in Gréalou, she entered a convent in the east just before World War One. During the war she served as a nurse's assistant. After the war she left the convent, came back here, and married a rascal who abandoned her after they had a child. Somehow, she had heard about a band of Aveyronais living in San Francisco. In the 1920s she left France and went to America, leaving her baby behind with my mother until she could get established. She began her life in San Francisco working in a laundry, then became a hotel clerk. When she overheard the owner of the hotel say he planned to sell his building, she persuaded him to sell it to her. She borrowed money to make the purchase and began. Not many years later, soldiers began returning by the thousands from World War Two. She had so much business she bought a second hotel."

Clare began to giggle as the old man told his story. "Both hotels are still in the family," she said.

"Oh! How do you know that?" asked the wife, now suddenly open and curious.

"Was her name Adele?" asked Clare.

"Yes, it was. How did you know?"

"She was my great grandmother. Her child was my grandmother, Nadine Marie."

The old man leaped up, hugged Clare, and sobbed, "Nadine took care of me when I was a baby. How can this be?"

"My name is Clarisse Adele Lanning. My mother Marie Annick is the daughter of Nadine Marie, who, of course, was the daughter of Adele Clarisse."

When the couple stopped weeping and finally settled back into their chairs, Clare traced the history of the family in America. When she finished, she added, "I have something to show you."

"What might this be?" asked the wife, wiping tears off her cheeks.

Clare reached into her backpack, pulled out her knife, and handed it to the old man.

"This is a soldier's knife. It became Adele's."

He looked down at the object in his palm and considered it for a long moment. "What does a soldier's knife have to do with Adele?"

"This knife belonged to an American."

"You mean she had an affair with an American while in the convent!" exclaimed his wife.

'No, no," responded Clare. "She knew the American only a few days before he died."

"Mother often said something deeply disturbing happened to her in the convent, but Adele never spoke of it."

"Even though it was only a short time, she was touched by him. I think meeting the American soldier caused her to dream."

"I don't understand. What does the knife have to do with all this?" asked the wife.

"A soldier's knife is a weapon of war, but for Adele it was an ironic symbol of a different life, of a life she imagined and longed for," Clare explained. She then recounted the story of Adele and the soldier. When she finished, the old man handed her the telephone, and the scene was replayed in San Francisco with as many tears there as had been shed in Gréalou.

Clare left the next morning, determined to be on her way. Sustained by croissants, coffee, and stories, she stepped out the front door and with a promise to keep in touch, started down the street. When she turned to wave and saw the couple standing on the front steps, she realized how difficult it must have been for the family to say goodbye, first to Adele and later to Nadine. At that moment her great grandmother Adele became family rather than ancestor.

Near the end of the morning, she came to a town with a weekly outdoor market still open for business. Never having been in a moving market, she decided to stroll through it and perhaps find something to eat. Expecting to see food vendors, she was surprised when the first stands she came to displayed low-price shoes, dresses, jeans, and accessories. She wandered among these stands, not interested in anything particular, but stopped at a table of belts and purses above which hung handbags attached to the outer edge of the canvas awning. Seeing the intricate, colorful patterns on the sides of the bags, she touched the soft leather and admired the designs. When the vendor asked what interested her, she said the bags were beautiful but had no need of one, and moved on.

Next to the stand of purses and handbags was a man sitting on a stool, reweaving seats of old wooden chairs with fresh new straw. He had either brought finished chairs from his workshop that morning or had worked steadily since arriving. Six neatly rewoven chairs stood in a straight row behind him waiting to be bought. She paused to watch the straw weaver at work and thought of the lacemaker in Le Puy. Although the weaver's labor was neither as complex nor as delicate as that of the lacemaker, his hands moved rapidly, and he too gazed casually at people passing by as he worked.

She passed the vendor of renovated chairs and moved into the heart of the market, where long white trailers stood end to end in irregular, parallel rows. A wall of each trailer was swung up and fixed horizontally in place creating a haphazard roof with the trailer on the opposite side. Vendors stood a little above customers, weighing and bagging produce or handing over purchased items. Older customers with little white-wheeled, plaid canvas shopping carts pointed to produce they wanted to buy or counted out change in their palms to pay for a purchase already made. Younger shoppers, carrying large bags or knapsacks, threaded their way carefully among the slower and less agile.

Clare stepped into a passageway, aromatic and colorful, and stopped at a fruit stand, where a white-haired woman with a five-euro note in hand waited as the vendor weighed and bagged her purchase. Clare squeezed in behind her, admiring apricots, cherries, melons, and pears, all laid out in neat rows and piles. When it was her turn, she bought two yellow pears, fruit she planned to eat soon because it did not transport well in a backpack.

Moving past the fruit stands, she came to a table of olives. The olive vendor, who had no customers at that moment, was barking out, "Spanish olives, try the olives, come taste the olives" with a North African accent. He looked at her as though anticipating a purchase, but she shook her head and continued, passing trays of green, black, and spicy olives mixed with slices of onions, peppers, and lemons. Beyond the olives were vegetable stands in front of which customers waited to buy locally grown zucchini, carrots, and leeks. Beyond the vegetables was a stand of carefully arranged bags of coarse sea salt and little wooden boxes heaped with mounds of ginger, sweet paprika, cumin, and coriander. She lingered to watch the spice seller, a woman in blue jeans and tee shirt, describe the ingredients of ras el hanout, a Moroccan mixture, to a shopper, then moved on.

Beyond the spices, she came to a small camping car where scissors and knives were sharpened and sold. Perched on a chair that swiveled from workbench to customer window, the vendor was sharpening a pair of scissors when Clare, attracted by the flickering sparks jetting off the stone wheel, stopped. Seeing her, he paused to ask if she would like to buy something. She said she had nothing to buy but wanted to have her knife sharpened. When she handed it to him, he was surprised to see an antique. Opening both ends of the knife, he said, "American, World War One."

"Yes, it is."

"Would you like to sell it?"

"No, no. It's a family heirloom. I just want to have it sharpened."

Studying the blade at one end and the spoon at the other, he said, "It hasn't had much hard use. I wouldn't sharpen it often." He then put the blade to the grindstone.

When finished, he folded the blade and spoon back into the handle and returned the knife. "That'll be five euros," he said. "You sure you don't want to sell it?"

"I'm sure," she said as she put it back into her pack and handed him five euros. "Thank you. Have a good day."

"You, too."

Leaving the knife sharpener, she chose an alley with cheese stands on one side and bread on the other. Since France produces more than three hundred different types of cheese, she was not surprised to see an extensive array of pressed, soft, and blue cheeses. She was tempted to buy a small chunk of cabécou, but not wanting to carry cheese in her pack, turned to breads on the opposite side of the passageway. With their various forms and golden colors, the breads were as enticing as the cheeses. Baguettes stood vertically on high, slatted shelves at the rear of the stand, and loaves and brioches lay behind glass on the front counter. Wanting something sweet, she got into line, bellied up against the display case and waited. As she inched toward the cash register, she noticed that no one spoke but all stood with money in hand, admiring the breads, ready to make their exchange. She did likewise.

When it was her turn, the vendor asked, "What can I get for you, Madame?"

"I would like a brioche, one with sugar on top."

When he reached for a large loaf, she said, "No, that one is too big. Give me a smaller one."

He chose one and put it into a sack. As he handed it across the counter to her, he cautioned, "I hope you aren't planning to put it into your backpack."

"No, I'm going to eat it before I get out of town," she said, then paid for her purchase and walked on.

The aroma of cooked meats began to mingle with that of breads and cheeses, and presently she came to stands with beef, pork, lamb, chicken, and duck. Cut meats hung neatly at the back, and baked meats, golden brown like the bread, lay behind glass at the front. Everything looked tasty and wonderful except a cow's tongue, gray and coarse, tucked in at the end of the counter.

She turned into a parallel, adjacent passage, where aromas of pork and poultry transformed into odors of the sea. In this passageway she saw boxes of gray oysters and red-headed fish, and beyond them, trays of shrimp, lobster, and crab, still clinging to life. Everything from the sea was lying in melting beds of ice that dripped into the street to form cold, malodorous puddles. Sea birds, standing nearby in open spaces, fought, unmindful of human traffic, for morsels that flew up when fish were hacked down to size. Skirting puddles and stepping around wet wheeled carts, she moved purposefully to the end of the passageway and out of the market.

At a pump she washed a pair of socks and a shirt, hung them on her backpack to dry, and sat on a nearby bench to eat lunch. She began with the soft brioche, savoring each bite, restraining herself from eating fast. When the sweet bread was gone, she grabbed a pear and began eating it. Soon the juice of the fruit ran across her fingers and dripped onto her legs. Not wanting to be bothered by flies during the afternoon, she stood up and bent slightly forward to finish the first and eat the second. After the pears were gone, she washed her hands and legs at the pump and returned to the bench.

While drying off in the sunlight, she saw a man with a cane shuffling laboriously toward her, hardly lifting his feet above the dead leaves on the trail. When he arrived, she carefully pulled her pack out of the way, and he sat down. He rested a few moments, gazing across the countryside as though lost in thought, then turned to look at her. His eyes were moist, the skin around them sagged. “I’m an American,” he said in fragile, raspy French. “My comrades and I were on patrol in a forest in southern Italy. We heard a child crying ahead of us on the trail, and when we found her, she said soldiers were hurting her mother. We picked her up and carried her back in the direction from which she came. When we saw the farmhouse, we set her in the underbrush and approached, not knowing who the soldiers were. We could hear a woman moan and the soldiers laugh. When we heard them speaking German, we burst through the door. Four soldiers were violating the woman. We shot one and forced the others out into the trees, where we shot them too. We left the woman and girl in the farmhouse and continued patrol. At the end of the war, I came back to look for them. The woman’s husband had been killed in the fighting. When I found her, we married, and I adopted her daughter. From Italy we migrated to France. I was a butcher here for forty years.” When the old man finished his tale, he paused, turned to look at Clare, and without another word hoisted himself up with help from her steadying hand and continued on his way. She watched him shuffle into the village.

The brutality of the tale had extinguished the tranquility of the bench and urged her to move on. Reaching into her pack, she pulled out the “Miam Miam Dodo” to see what lay ahead and was pleased to see that the trail became a Roman road farther west. She returned the guide to her pack, and began walking, putting the old man’s tale out of her mind and looking forward to a wide, straight thoroughfare. A couple of hours later she passed a marker indicating the beginning of the Roman road and was disappointed to see this segment of the trail wasn't any different from what she had been taking for days.

Although the road did not exist as she had imagined, it seemed eerie to be walking where soldiers had marched two thousand years before. She heard the tramp of booted feet, quiet conversations, and the whinny of horses, as tired fighters trudged resolutely to their camp before the next battle with tribal warriors. On the chariots and shields she saw images of an eagle and braided wheat, symbols of the power and prosperity of a great civilization.

By the time the Romans arrived in the region, the first walkers had long disappeared in antiquity, but like the Romans, they too used a symbol to identify and express themselves. Instead of evoking power and prosperity, their symbol, a simple clam shell with converging ridges, represented an eternal, life-giving sun that bathed itself each evening in the west and rose the next morning in the east to refresh the earth.

Late in the eighth century, hundreds of years after the end of the Roman Empire, Christians, wanting to drive the Moors out of Spain, began a long war. Early in the ninth century they found the bones of a man in a crypt and called them the bones of Saint James. When word spread east that James's bones had been enshrined near the western tip of Spain, the effect was to rally Christians in the conflict and attract other Christians from throughout Europe. When arriving to support their fellow believers, they chose the first walkers' shell as their symbol but gave it a different meaning. Rather than suggesting simplicity and purification, it symbolized the power and authority of a religion.

Clare realized that some present-day hikers maintained the tradition of the clam shell, either as a tribute to early walkers or as a symbol of Christian belief. Whether carrying a shell or not, hikers had many reasons for walking. Some were motivated by religious conviction, others by a passion for nature, and others by interest in the trail culture. But there were hikers who had more complex reasons for walking. Clare heard of a bus driver who was involved in a dreadful accident while bringing children to school. One of the children was killed and others were injured. Although not at fault, the driver shouldered a heavy sack of guilt and carried it to Santiago to deal with her burden and find a reason to live.

Clare had seen an American movie entitled *The Way.* Directed by Emilio Estevez, it was about four people who met by chance on the trail and eventually walked together. Troubled by events in their lives, they all sought tranquility. The only woman in the group, a Canadian, had been abused by a man and aborted her baby girl because of fear and anger. An annoying Hollander wanted to lose weight because his wife was unhappy with him, and he was probably unhappy with himself. An Irishman, a blocked writer, hoped to recover his muse, and an American doctor planned to scatter the ashes of his son, who had died on the trail across the Pyrenees, along the way.

Clare saw Estevez's movie as a story of exploration, not exploration of a country but of the human condition, and the trail was the means by which his characters searched for a way to move on. The American, who had rejected his son, struggled to forgive himself. The woman confronted her guilt and abuse, and the blocked writer, liberated by his walk, reacquired his gift. The fat Hollander did not change his habit of overeating, but he became more sensitive and less annoying to his fellow hikers. Each hiker stopped at the shrine, then continued walking beyond it to the sea, accepting his or her own past, imperfect as it was, and left the sea, looking forward to the future, imperfect as it might be. They were not pilgrims going to honor the past and affirm belief in the dry bones of a saint. Rather, they were like the first walkers who walked to the sea to absorb the regenerating power of the sun, and like Terry Fox who ran west to honor life.

At the edge of a village, she came to an intriguing structure she recognized from photos and paintings but had never actually seen. It was a lavoire, an ancient, outdoor public laundry, where women gathered with friends to wash clothes and visit. If they hadn't been destroyed by time and war, lavoires had been transformed into ponds and pools for animals and tourists. This one had become a home for ducks.

She dropped her pack to the ground, sat on the surrounding stone wall, and looked down at the water.

When the birds saw her sitting there, they gathered in the shadows hoping for a handout. Unable to resist their murmuring requests, she took a dry, demi-baguette from her backpack, tore it into pieces, and threw them into the water. This gesture shattered the late afternoon calm and ignited a storm of quacks and squawks as though the birds hadn't eaten for days. Because the baguette was small, and the ducks were numerous, the impromptu feast soon came to an end, and the birds, realizing there was nothing more, paddled away. When calm and quiet returned, she sat a few moments more, then slid off the stone wall and walked into the hamlet.

Near the center of the village, she found a restaurant and entered. At this early time of evening, diners were few, and she had her choice of tables. She picked a table along a far wall and sat facing the front door and bar. While she waited for service, two men carrying backpacks came through the door and looked over the room. Seeing her sitting next to a pack of her own, they approached.

"Bonsoir, Madame. May we join you?" asked the older man.

"Yes, of course," she replied.

The men, tall and angular, set their packs down, pulled out chairs, and sat across from her.

Before they could introduce themselves, the waiter arrived, set a bottle of rosé du Tarn on the table along with a basket of bread, and suggested the special of the evening, Artichauts à la Grecque as the entrée, Gratin Méridional as the main dish, and Flan Mirabelles for dessert.

"How big are the portions?" asked the younger of the two men.

"Big enough for hikers," said the waiter in an exchange that had now become familiar to Clare.

Hearing that response, she and her dining companions ordered what had been proposed, and the waiter returned to the kitchen.

The older man turned their glasses upright and poured wine.

"You are one of us?" asked the younger.

"If you mean hiker, yes, I am. My name is Clare."

"I'm Edorto. My uncle here, his name is Balendin. We come from the Basque region of Spain."

"I'm from the United States."

When Edorto heard that Clare was an American, he switched to well-polished English. "I went to high school for a year in Massachusetts. Everybody there called me Ed."

"How was life at a school in Massachusetts?"

"I played a lot of soccer. The sport was new at the school. I had been playing since I was six-years-old, so I became a junior coach on the team as well as player."

Falling under the charm of this handsome young man, Clare playfully asked, "Did you do anything besides play sports in Massachusetts?"

Sensing mild sarcasm, Edorto replied in like manner. "Yes, of course. I went to classes, although I don't remember which ones. I do remember the girls, though. They were pretty."

"You sound like a typical American male high school student."

"That's what I wanted to be. Actually, I was a good student. My father and mother would have been quite displeased if I had been a negligent one. And I probably wouldn't be taking the trail now."

"How's that?"

"My favorite class was science. For part of the year, we studied geology which led me into my career."

"Which is?"

"I'm in the petroleum business. Some day I would like to work for a company in the States."

The conversation was interrupted when the waiter arrived with the entrée, bowls of artichokes resting on a layer lettuce, olives, and feta.

After sampling the dish, Edorto asked, "I like the spices. What are they?"

The waiter replied, "The usual, garlic, coriander, cumin, rosemary and a Brazilian spice known only to the cook."

Balendin poured more wine, and everyone reached into the basket for a chunk of baguette and began eating.

Clare turned to the old man and in French said, "I assume you are retired."

"No, no, I'm not retired. I have a little apple orchard and a cider house. We are in the slow season now so I'm taking a little time off."

"I am not familiar with cider houses."

"Cider houses are buildings where apple juice is fermented and stored in big wooden casks."

"Like a winery?"

"More or less, yes. During the winter when the cider is ready, we put up tables and serve lunch. When diners want to drink, they get up, put their glasses under a spigot in a barrel and catch the new cider. At that time of year, we are quite busy."

"I suppose Basque food is different from French or Spanish food."

"It's basically a mixture of Spanish, French, and traditional Basque cuisine, mostly sea food, lamb and vegetables. A typical lunch at our place would be a salad, an omelet with pieces of cod in it, and a ragu of lamb. For dessert we might serve brioche with jam, or yogurt, usually something simple."

After the entrée, the waiter returned with an artfully arranged platter of sliced tomatoes, zucchini, eggplant, and chopped onions, sautéed in olive oil and seasoned with salt, pepper and herbes de Provence. The hikers each grabbed another chunk of bread, took a moment to comment on the pleasant odor of the vegetables and on the elegance of the presentation, then helped themselves.

"I don't know anything about Basque country or customs," said Clare.

"The Basque region is in the north of the Pyrenees. If you keep walking west, you'll climb the Pyrenees and come to it."

"I plan to do that next summer. Is it dangerous?"

"Summers can be dangerous because of big changes in temperature. They can be hot during the day and cold at night. This causes dense fogs and mists in the morning, and if hikers aren't paying attention, they sometimes fall over a cliff. Winters have avalanches that can be treacherous, especially for skiers who leave established trails or who ski too late in the day."

"I mean Basque country. Is it dangerous to walk through?" repeated Clare.

"Other than the mountains, Basque country is not particularly dangerous," noted Balendin, a little annoyed by the implication of the question.

Sensing his tone of voice, Clare replied diffidently, "I thought the Basques wanted to separate from Spain."

Despite his annoyance, he smiled and replied softly with a question of his own, "Do you think the Basques are dangerous people, perhaps bombers and terrorists?"

"I've heard they are a tough, exacting people who want their independence."

"For years, the Basque language was banned, institutions and organizations suppressed, and people were tortured. Thousands were forced into exile. After years of fighting, we finally became semi-autonomous in 1978, but we still do not have the status of nation. How did you Americans get your independence? You got it by agitating and fighting, no?"

As though trying to excuse the annoyance of his uncle, Edorto added, "Our culture is unique. We are a distinct people with our own language and ethnicity, and it is difficult to tolerate intrusions and restrictions."

"This is the fourth time I have walked the Camino," said Balendin.

Clare wanted to ask Balendin why he was taking the Camino again, but sensing his agitation, she changed the subject slightly. "Why are you so far east of the Pyrenees when Santiago is west of the mountains?"

"We are walking east to Conques," Edorto answered. "At Conques I must leave for Paris on business, and my uncle will turn around and walk back by himself."

"Which route would you suggest I take when crossing Spain next summer?"

"I suggest you stay along the north coast," replied Balendin. "If you take a trail farther south, the temperature will rise to more than 120 degrees. The coast is not always picturesque. You will be walking near busy highways and crossing industrial zones, and you may have to take a ferry or train for a short distance, but the weather will be more tolerable."

Seeing the northern route from a somewhat different point of view, Edorto added, "Buy a bikini. Some beaches along the north coast are very pleasant." Then to Clare's surprise and pleasure, he asked, "By the way, do you mind giving me your telephone number in the States? I go there from time to time on business."

While the Basques described what lay ahead for Clare, the waiter cleared the table and returned with dessert, a flan of yellow mirabelle plums. When Clare asked the waiter how the dessert was made, Balendin interrupted, "It's baked in a batter of flour, eggs, milk, and butter, and seasoned with eau-de-vie de Mirabelles," and Edorto added, "Eau-de-vie gives plums a slightly tart taste." When the flan was finished, they ordered coffee, and while waiting for it to arrive, Clare wrote her phone number on a napkin and handed it to Edorto.

Pigs and Pilgrims

Clare wished the Basques good luck and left the restaurant, hoping to meet Edorto again. She was, however, thinking more about Balendin than about his nephew at that moment. There was something enigmatic about the old man. He was taking the trail a fourth time, he had said. She knew that some hikers become obsessed by the trail, and they return to it whenever they can, but she did not think this was his reason for walking again. Perhaps he wanted to make amends for his rebellious attitudes and those of his people, and his walk was a form of compensation, but she rejected this reasoning because he had made it quite clear the Basques were fighting for their rights. What crime was there in wanting independence and fighting for it, he had asked, and cited the Americans, pointing out what greatness their independence had brought them. Perhaps, she concluded, he was like the hikers in the Estevez movie, who by taking the trail had learned to face unhappy situations and get on with their lives.

When coming to a small hill, she decided to camp above the trail amongst the trees. She scrambled steeply upward through heavy underbrush that bordered the trail, and when emerging from the dense vegetation on the upper side, continued climbing until the hill levelled out slightly. She set up her tent among the trees, prepared for bed, and was about to settle in for the night when she realized her water bottle was missing. Thinking she had lost it in the underbrush and not wanting spend time in the morning looking for it, she put her boots back on, descended, and began pawing through the undergrowth. Impatient to find the bottle before nightfall, she paused to look up and down the darkening trail. Luckily, she did that. To her surprise, she saw the healer in the near distance coming toward her in the semi-darkness. This time she remained steady. Hidden by the bushes, she watched him approach, saw his head bob past just below, then watched him walk beyond into the enveloping darkness of the trail.

She rose with as little noise as possible, abandoned her search for the water bottle, and retreated to the camp above. She thought it wise to sleep elsewhere that night, for if he had seen her and found the tent, there would be no chance of escape. She grabbed the sleeping bag, pillow, and knife, and hastily climbed higher up the hill until finding a clear, flat spot well above the tent. Hoping it wouldn't rain during the night, she laid out the bag, put the pillow on top, and set the knife next to it. Taking off her boots a second time, she slid into the bag and waited for sleep that did not come until well after midnight. When it finally arrived, the Healer stepped off the trail, climbed the hill, and crept into her dreams.

The next morning her dreams seemed to transmute into reality when she was slammed awake. She had turned over onto her stomach during the night, drawn her hands into the bag to keep warm, and was now being rolled in the dirt away from her knife. She twisted her body to claw at the bag's zipper, but before finding it, was lifted and dropped to the ground a second time, with a blow that knocked the breath out of her. Disoriented but determined to liberate herself, she struggled until finally grasping the zipper and slithering out of the bag. On hands and knees, she searched for the knife, but foundering in soft dirt and unable to find it, turned toward her assailant and lifted her arms to protect herself.

She had never particularly liked pigs, but now suddenly felt a curious affection for them. A wild pig searching for grubs and acorns had wandered with her shoats into the camp and was rooting in the dirt around the sleeping bag. With her thick, muscular neck and strong snout, she had rolled Clare over and lifted the bag, hoping to find something to eat under it. Trying to be unobtrusive and non-threatening, Clare settled into the pig-plowed dirt and watched patiently as the family searched for whatever morsel they could find around her. It was amusing to see the tan, striped, little piglets, their curved tails twitching nervously, moving intently about the camp as though she didn't exist, sniffing and rooting, fighting with brothers and sisters for whatever tidbit they turned up. When mother and offspring had eaten all the grubs, nuts, and mushrooms they could find, they drifted into another part of the forest and disappeared.

While sitting in the soft, black dirt, she put on her boots. Then retrieving her knife, she picked up the bag and pillow and cautiously descended to the lower camp. Thinking the healer might be inside the tent, she crouched behind a cluster of bushes and waited with open knife in hand until the sun was well above the horizon. When her patience came to an end, she tiptoed to the tent and peeked in. It was empty.

She packed her equipment, ate trail mix, and descended, finding her water bottle under a bush on the way down. She had hoped to awaken ready for a long day of walking, but the pig incident, curious as it was, combined with her agitation at seeing the healer, made her feel drained and weary. She set warily off on the trail. When coming to a stream, she followed it away from the trail to a clump of trees. Out of sight she bathed her face and feet in the cold spring water, washed a pair of socks, and started off again, now looking forward to food, a hot shower, and a warm bed.

Walking calmed her down and raised her confidence. Amused by the pig incident, she thought about the interaction of humans and wild animals along the trail. She wondered what early walkers would have done if pigs had wandered into their camp, but soon realized this way of thinking was pointless. She knew what their reaction would have been. Instead of seeing pigs as intruders, they would have welcomed them as unexpected gifts.

One of the walkers catches a screaming, kicking shoat, pulls it up to his chest with one hand, and deftly slits

its throat with a sharpened flint in the other. While hot blood squirts from the animal's neck, other walkers gather dry wood and start a fire. The shoat is skewered with a sturdy, pointed stick and hung between two forked stakes above the flames. Everyone fans out to look for fruit of the forest and returns with hands full of acorns, hickory nuts, walnuts, mushrooms, and grubs. They sit around the fire, sing songs, tell stories, and wait patiently as the hide blackens and fat drips into the flames. When the piglet is roasted, they throw nuts into the coals and lay the mushrooms and grubs along the edge. Nuts crack in the intense heat, mushrooms turn brown, and insects squirm in a dance of death. As the piglet is slid off the skewer and cut into pieces, the mushrooms and grubs are picked carefully from the ashes, and nuts are fished one by one from the coals. By now everyone has a crude bowl in hand and is ready to eat.

As much as she felt close to her early, imaginary walkers, Clare knew she was quite unlike them in the matter of eating. She did not like killing animals and preferred to eat a chicken leg or a slice of pork without thinking about how it got from pen or pasture to plate. But she realized that death was part of the journey. First walkers killed and butchered animals along the way to feed and protect themselves, and animals killed humans for the same reasons. In the evolution of creatures on Earth, this process seemed natural enough, although distasteful to her modern way of delicate thinking.

Killing for food led her to think about killing for other reasons, reasons that were quite unnatural to her and had nothing to do with the real need for survival. This killing, driven by desire to dominate or by fear of difference, was cloaked in the costume of righteous authority and disguised in moral principle. She recalled the museum version of the Beast of Gévaudan, a dark and sinister tale in which religion exploited the fear and ignorance of peasants. And she thought about the American soldier, whose knife she carried. His life and the lives of thousands of soldiers on both sides of the Great War had been wasted because of fear, unyielding beliefs, and the inflexible attitudes of politically and religiously powerful men.

Late in the morning she noticed an inconspicuous gite sign nailed to a tree and pointing to a path into a valley. She turned off the trail and took the path. Oddly, it was bordered on both sides by plants with labels indicating species and genus, making her feel as though she were descending into a botanical garden. At the bottom she came a spacious, well-manicured lawn surrounding a barn and large, renovated house. She crossed the lawn, knocked on the door, and was greeted by a friendly but frazzled woman with a baby in her arms. She asked if she could get something to eat and stay the night, but the woman replied that dinner would not be served until eight and every bed was taken. She added, though, that Clare was welcomed to relax at a table on the lawn.

Disappointed, Clare decided to stop only long enough to eat her remaining food. She sat under a large elm and, sorry to have given the ducks the last of her baguette, opened her backpack. She had eaten the trail mix that morning but found an orange and a sack containing a negligent mixture of cashews and dates. Although the orange was soft, and the dates had acquired the salty taste of nuts, she was pleased to have something to eat.

While eating she watched a man with curly gray hair and short white beard working on a project near the barn. Smoking a pipe clenched tightly between his teeth, he was meticulously painting the name of the gite on a large, weather-worn, oval sign that had originally been made for some other business. When he'd finished, he set the sign against the wall of the barn, took the pipe from his mouth, and with a critical eye stepped back to look at his work. After a touchup here and there, he cleaned his brushes and put them in a well-worn toolbox. Seeing Clare on the other side of the lawn, he said, "Bonjour, I bet my daughter told you the gite is full."

"Bonjour, Monsieur. Yes, she did. So, I need to keep walking."

"Are you going east or west?"

"I'm going west."

"Then I would recommend the pilgrims' house at Cahors."

"I usually sleep in my tent, but sometimes I need a break from camping. What's a pilgrim's house?"

The man approached the table with a slight limp and sat down across from her. "Pilgrims' houses," he said, "are ordinary houses usually owned by religious organizations that provide hikers with a place to eat and sleep. They are staffed by volunteers who greet hikers, make meals, wash bedding, and clean up after everyone has left in the morning."

"I see that hosting hikers is not an easy task."

"I think my daughter would agree with you there. She and her husband work ten hours a day, six days a week. A pilgrim's house is a good place to stay because volunteers are conscientious."

"Living close to the trail, you must be a hiker."

"I don't live out here in the country, but I like hiking."

"So, you've been to the shrine in Santiago?"

"I've been to Santiago but never to the shrine."

"Why is that?"

"It's a story of immigration and displacement," he said, as though describing a novel. He then switched to a personal level. "My father was born in Spain, my mother in France. We were living in Spain during the civil war. I was a child at that time. When the government discovered my father was in the Resistance, my mother and I were put in an internment camp. There I was abused by the nuns and lost hearing in one ear when cuffed by a priest who supported Franco. These people were not good people."

"I see you are a botanist."

"Oh, you noticed my tags. I'm not really a botanist, well, perhaps an amateur one. I was a university history professor. Now I am retired."

"You keep busy with botany?"

"That's one of my projects. I also study with a local astronomy club, and I read books written in Occitan."

"I remember an owner of a gite where I stayed. He spoke with an accent I had never heard before, a little like yours."

"It was probably Occitan, a descendent of Latin that people call langue d'oc. It's still spoken in Spain and Italy but hardly at all in France. It was a common language here in the south until a French minister by the name of Jules Ferry succeeded in prohibiting its teaching in public schools in the 1950s. You can still hear a few of the older people speak it, and you might hear French spoken with an Occitan accent now and then, but the language is almost dead here in France."

"The same thing happened to Native Americans," replied Clare. "Indian children were taken from families, sent to boarding schools, and forbidden to speak their native language during the late nineteenth and early twentieth centuries. Their languages have disappeared or are close to extinction. American culture and American English would be richer if these languages were still spoken."

"Language control is not unusual in France. We have a group of intellectuals called the French Academy, which has been in existence for four hundred years. Its influence on grammar and vocabulary has limited the agility and breadth of the language and has retarded its evolution. I'm sure the Academy supported Ferry's decision to extinguish Occitan. It gives me great pleasure to see technical computer English drift into the French language. Since you camp, you probably stargaze from time to time."

"It's difficult to ignore the heavens when camping."

"Summer is a good time to look for constellations. During much of the year clouds come up from the southern Atlantic or down from Scandinavia, and we often have overcast night skies. But during mid-summer, the sky is clearer."

"I can identity the Big Dipper and the North Star, but they are the only stars I recognize easily."

"The Big Dipper, as you call it in English, is part of the constellation Ursa Major. Where are you from?"

"I'm from the north central region of the United States."

"Then you've seen the same constellations we see here in southern France. We're at approximately the same latitude as the northern part of the United States.

"I suppose I've seen a few, but I don't know any of their names."

"I have a pile of star maps in my car that illustrate the northern constellations. We use them when teaching astronomy classes at schools and conferences. If you have a few minutes, I'll get one for you."

"That depends on how far Cahors is from here."

"You will have no problem reaching Cahors by late afternoon. I'll get you a map."

When he returned, the professor flattened the poster out on the table, and beginning with Ursa Major delineated the shapes of constellations around it and explained the origin and meaning of their mythological names. He was about to go on to more distant constellations but seeing fatigue and confusion in Clare's eyes, stopped and said, "Too bad the gite is full. If you were to stay a day or two, I could teach you much about the northern sky." Folding the map, he handed it to her. "When you're sitting in a cafe, take this out and study it, and just before crawling into your tent at night, locate a constellation or two."

"I will have many nights to get acquainted with the stars," said Clare as she tucked the map into her pack. "Now I must leave for Cahors."

"When you get into town, ask for directions to the pilgrim's house. It will be easy enough to find. But before you go, I want to tell you something about the city, so you'll know what to expect when you arrive."

Intrigued, Clare paused.

"During the Middle Ages Cahors was infamous for bankers who charged interest on loans. This practice was strictly forbidden by the Church, and because of it, the city became known as a sinful pit of usury and extortion and was considered so wicked Dante mentioned it with Sodom and Gomorrah in the *Inferno*. Be careful when you enter the city."

Although the professor was smiling as he cautioned her, Clare didn't know whether to take him seriously, but assumed she would find out when arriving. She shook his hand, thanked him for the poster, and walked up the hill through the tagged forest out to the trail.

Land along the way looked as though it were still cursed for the sins of the bankers. Here and there the earth was parched and stony, and the cedar forests, if one could call them that, were scrubby and sparse. Strangely she noticed small patches of vigorous, neatly aligned oak trees, which made her wonder why anyone would bother planting oaks on rock-strewn hills in the middle of scrub forests. Occasionally she saw signs advertising dog training and competition, but never saw a dog.

Well before Cahors, she was surprised to come upon a neatly tended soccer field within a forest. At the far end of the field under a clump of tall trees stood a long, narrow shed with the sign Club House Café painted on its wall in bright red letters. Nearby were white tables and chairs partially hidden in the shade of trees. Walking along the edge of the field, she assumed the cafe was there to serve spectators during soccer matches and suspected it was nothing more than a bar with alcohol, coffee, chips, and nuts. When she passed the front door and discovered the cafe open, she turned off the trail and despite her doubts sat at a table.

The barman came out and handed her a menu, which confirmed her suspicion. There were wines, whiskies, beer, sodas, and coffee to drink, and nuts and chips to eat. Having nothing else to choose from, she asked for a cup of coffee and peanuts. While the barman was gone, she looked across the field, wondering where teams that competed in it came from, and when he returned, he explained they were regional amateur teams that competed on weekends. She then asked about the cultivated oak trees along the trail. He replied that the patches she had seen were truffle plots. Farmers planted rows of oak trees, tended them for fifteen years, then harvested truffles among the roots until the fungus diminished, and new oaks had to be planted in another location.

She assumed the barman would go back to work, but since she was the only customer, and he had nothing else to do, he put one foot up on a chair and began talking about his experiences with hikers. Although an accountant by profession, he was a psychologist, sociologist, and humanitarian at the Club House Café. He had served patrons from as far away as Quebec, Australia, and Japan and talked about them so vividly she imagined they had just left the bar and were not far down the trail. Recently he received a marriage announcement from a Swiss woman and a New Zealander, who had met at the cafe. Attached was a note saying they were coming back to see him soon. He let a penniless young man stay in a storage shed behind the cafe, and was paid with a bouquet of wildflowers lying on the doorstep of the bar the next morning. He encouraged a walker who had lost her son to keep moving on, and had urged another walker to stop and go home.

Clare became so engrossed in these imaginative descriptions of passing humanity that she hardly noticed other hikers arriving, and presently there was an audience of a half-dozen sitting behind her listening attentively, waiting patiently to be served. When he finished his monologue, which by the end had become a bit theatrical, the barman took his foot off the chair, left his imaginary stage, and moved about his audience to take orders.

Inclined to stay longer, but needing to reach Cahors early enough to get a bed, Clare laid money for the coffee and peanuts on the table and got up to leave. When she turned to pick up her pack, the pleasant ambiance of the cafe suddenly turned sour. The healer was sitting just behind her, so close he could have stroked her hair or run the tips of his fingers up and down the back of her uncovered arm. As she arched her back to hoist the pack to her shoulders, he gazed at her breasts and smiled benignly. If thinking clearly, she would have asked the barman for help, but instead she lurched past him and hurried across the lawn to the trail, almost knocking a customer out of his chair as she left.

She walked at an agitated pace for several miles, turning from time to time to see if the healer were following. When no one came into view behind her, she finally slowed down, gained a bit of confidence, and started thinking about how she had gotten locked into a relationship with this man. Many women walked the trail, and he must have encountered some of them, but since he was not known by the trail grapevine, he had remained relatively inconspicuous. She had started out badly with him. She should have ignored his request to heal her in the first place or given him money and been done with it. But in some way, she had opened the door to him, and since that first encounter, he had come in with a swaggering, invasive manner she could not tolerate.

By leaving the Club House Café as she had, she had acted like the helpless peasant women in the museum version of the Beast of Gévaudan, who believed they had no possibility of escape if they encountered the wolf. She did not like this benighted submissiveness, and as she calmed down, began to hear the woman in the green statue speak to her, urging her to straighten up.

Cahors, City of the Devil

Arriving at Cahors late in the day, she stopped at a tabac to enquire about the pilgrims' house. The man behind the counter replied she was almost there, then going to a window, pointed to a big white house standing alone across the street a little farther on. At the door of the house, she was greeted by Didier, a retired businessman from eastern France who was in his last full day of volunteering. When he said a bed was available, she cleaned up, washed clothes, and settled into a comfortable living room chair to visit with other arrivals.

During dinner that evening Didier told his guests he planned to leave the next day and travel. His plan was to fly to Montreal, buy a BMW motorcycle, and ride across Canada up to Anchorage, Alaska. From Anchorage he would go south along the west coast to the tip of South America. Clare thought this was an ambitious plan for someone who had been born just after World War Two.

The sun was pawing at the east windows wanting to get in when she awoke the next morning. The mood at breakfast was cheerful, and everyone, whether going east or west, looked forward to a good day on the trail. Happy to be leaving the burdens of housekeeping to his replacement, Didier was upbeat as well. While listening to hikers at the breakfast table talk about what lay ahead, he couldn't resist cautioning westward walkers about a bridge they would soon cross on their way out of the city.

"You will soon come to Pont Valentré, a handsome five-arched bridge built in the fourteenth century. Folklore says that construction of this bridge took decades because every time it was almost finished, someone dismantled it, and workers had to start over. Finally, the exasperated master builder made a pact with the devil. If the devil helped him finish the project, the builder would give him his soul. The pact was concluded, and construction began again. But when the bridge was almost finished, the builder could not bear giving up his soul and concocted a scheme. He asked the devil to lay the last stone. When the fiend agreed, the builder gave him a sieve instead of a pail to carry water for making mortar. This situation, of course, stopped the completion of the bridge, saved the master builder's soul, and frustrated the devil forever after."

"He wasn't a very intelligent devil," said an amused hiker.

"Yes, devils weren't very intelligent in those days," agreed Didier.

He then finished his story with a bit of advice. "When you cross the bridge, look up at the last tower. There you will see the devil. But don't smile and certainly don't wave at him. You never know what he might do."

In the bright morning sunlight, the calm waters of the Lot reflected the beauty and grace of roses growing along the levee's edge, and in the distance Pont Valentré appeared as elegant and graceful as the flowers. When Clare arrived at the bridge and began crossing, she stopped in the middle and looked up. Clinging to the corner of the farthest tower was the frustrated devil. Made of cement himself, he was looking off into the distance, perhaps wondering if the last stone would ever be cemented in. Remembering the words of Didier but wanting to be mockingly contrary, she smiled and waved, then passed under the tragi-comic figure and crossed to the other side of the river.

Beyond the bridge the trail steepened considerably. Struggling up a flight of large stone blocks planted by nature, she felt as though she had left the realm of the devil and entered the kingdom of a giant. The ascent was short in distance but long in time. At the top she turned to look down on the devilish bridge and the infamous city. Both seemed calm and agreeable even though bankers still charged interest and the devil remained high up on the tower, looking as displeased as ever. A little farther on, she saw expensive, solar-paneled homes perched on rocky slopes, from which the view of the Lot Valley must have been magnificent. In the sand she spotted a dead cicada. Considering all the noise cicadas make, she thought this insect was not very impressive, mostly gray wings.

During the morning she came upon a couple with two adolescent daughters. "Bonjour," she said, hailing them from a distance. Turning in unison to see who was approaching, they replied, "Bonjour, Madame," and waited for her to catch up.

"May I walk with you a while?" Clare asked.

"Certainly," replied the father. "The trail is big enough for everyone."

"What did you think of the climb out of Cahors?" Clare asked the girls.

"I felt like a very tiny person trying to climb a gigantic stairway," responded the younger of the two. "Did you see the devil on the tower?"

"I did. I even waved at him."

"You did! Did he frown at you?"

"Not that I noticed. He seemed to be looking off in the distance. I wonder what he was thinking."

"He looked rather crabby," noted the older sister.

"Pont Valentré is a very beautiful bridge," said the mother. "When we approached the city from the mountain, we watched a train move slowly on the levee. It turned to cross the river on a bridge. Luckily, it wasn't the Valentré. A railroad track across that bridge would have spoiled it."

"What's your name?" asked the older girl.

"My name is Clare. What's yours?"

"I'm Mégalie. Where are you from?"

"I'm from America."

"I'm studying English," said Mégalie. "I took a national English test this spring. Sixteen thousand six hundred and sixty-four people took the test, and I was number one hundred and seventy."

"You must be very good in English to be in the top ten percent."

"I wasn't in the top ten percent."

"You weren't?"

"No, I was in the top one percent, or almost the top one percent."

"Well, congratulations on all your hard work."

"I play the ukulele and write songs in French and English, and I'm on a rowing team." Putting one foot forward to show her leg, Mégalie said, "I have strong thighs and good wind. We go to regional competitions, and we usually win."

Clare turned to the younger girl and asked, "What is your name?"

"Elise. I'm eleven, and I play basketball."

"I play basketball too," said Clare. "What position do you play?"

"I'm good at dribbling and passing so the coach made me point guard. I play on a boys' team, and I start. What position do you play?"

"I play forward on a girls' team," responded Clare.

"We went to America when Papa ran in the New York marathon. He's a good runner," said Mégalie.

"Out of one hundred thousand applicants only thirty thousand were accepted. When I decided to run, the French quota was filled, so I couldn't get a French permit. Luckily, I have a sister living in Mexico. Somehow her husband got a Mexican permit for me," said the father.

"So, you were a French runner running in an American race with Mexican colors."

"And I finished in less than three hours," concluded the father proudly.

"Did you have a good time in New York?" Clare asked the girls.

"Oh, yes, we did. We saw the Statue of Liberty, went to a big zoo, and had a picnic in Central Park. Did you know that the Statue of Liberty was given to the Americans by the French?"

"No, I didn't know that."

"It was supposed to be a centennial present, but it arrived a little late."

"I'm sure being late didn't matter. It was the thought that counted."

Clare spent the morning with the family, chatting about whatever came to the girls' minds, but when they came to a village, she decided to stop for lunch. The girls, disappointed to see her leave, gave her a regretful hug, and said goodbye. Their parents shook her hand and wished her "bonne continuation."

"It was my pleasure," said Clare. "Good luck with rowing and basketball." She then turned toward the village and left the family.

She found a grocery store/cafe, bought a sandwich, fries, salad, and apple pie, and found a table on the terrace. While eating, she thought about the girls she had walked with that morning, wondering if American children would be as tolerant of walking with their parents. She remembered seeing a father and his teenage son taking the trail on mountain bikes. The boy must have had an attitude like that of the girls. Riding hour after hour with a parent and pushing a loaded bicycle over hills and across streams required patience and tolerance as well as physical endurance.

As she was reflecting on these sturdy children, two young men, looking insolent and dissipated, ambled through the store and came out to the patio. Dressed in shabby military pants tucked into dirty boots and carrying large, ragged packs, each one was trailing a scrawny dog as ill-kempt and brazen appearing as its master. They tied their dogs to a table leg at the far end of the patio, returned to the store, and began making rounds among the shelves. Each bought a bottle of wine and came out to sit at their table. One opened the bottles with an opener stashed in his back pocket, while the other pulled paper and a small bag of pot from a shirt pocket and prepared a smoke. He lined the pot along the paper, rolled the paper into a tube, and sealed it with his tongue. Striking a match, he lit the joint, inhaled deeply, and handed it to his buddy.

Clare had finished her sandwich and fries and was tranquilly eating the salad when she heard one of the men say, "You want to have some fun with us, Madame? Come over and take some wine. Maybe you would like to smoke a little, too."

"No, thank you," she replied, trying to project a neutral voice.

But her response was a challenge to the other one. "This is a nice day for some fun. Come here, try it," he persisted, holding up the joint.

"No, I am not interested," she responded.

"You must be from Holland. I've heard Dutch girls like to smoke and make love. Is this so?"

"I wouldn't know," said Clare.

"Are you taking the trail? Maybe we could walk with you this afternoon and find a place to camp," said the other.

"You think she's got a big tent?"

"I am sure she has a big tent but not that big. We could take turns, you and me, sleeping in it."

"I think she is a mademoiselle. She looks too fresh to be a madame."

Clare held firm under this barrage of derision but got fed up with it. She wanted to push her apple pie into the face of one and slap the other, but thinking they might follow her into the country and retaliate, she left the pie, picked up her sticks and bag, and went to the bathroom. When she opened the door and peaked out across the patio a short time later, the degenerates, intensely consumed by pleasures of the moment, had forgotten her. She hurried to the counter, paid her bill, and walked out the back door into the fresh air of the countryside. While she didn't feel overwhelmed by these potheads, her experience with them rekindled an uneasiness that had been dormant in the morning.

This vague disquiet stayed with her during the afternoon, and she walked robotically like the mules in the coal mines of Decazeville. Toward the end of the day this inattentiveness turned into focused alarm when she saw the silhouette of a man on his knees farther up the trail. She halted and squinted against the sun. From where she stood, this man could have been the healer looking for something in the weeds or a devout pilgrim praying for something in the heavens. Not wanting to detour through unknown country or retreat and possibly meet the potheads, she forced herself to approach, hoping he wouldn't look up before she could determine whether to stay or flee. Fortunately, he was intensely engrossed in his activity, and when getting near, she saw this man was neither healer nor pilgrim, only a farmer repairing a fence.

"Bonjour, Monsieur," she said.

Taking a nail from between his lips, the farmer turned, considered Clare for an instant, and replied engagingly, "Bonjour, Madame."

"You have beautiful horses," said Clare with relief as she looked across the pasture.

"Thank you. People rent them to take the trail. Would you like to rent one?"

"No thanks," she said, sensing an amusingly sarcastic yet comforting attitude in this man. "I prefer walking. I haven't seen any horses along the way, but I've noticed a few mules."

"Horses are easier to manage. They're not so independent and stubborn."

"So, you're a Texas-type rancher."

"My ranch is pretty small compared to those in Texas, but it's big enough to raise a few horses. Did you know these animals are quite intelligent? Mules, donkeys, and horses have a remarkable memory for direction. After only one trip along the trail, they can find their way home, even in the dark. That's a good trait to have when some of those inept hikers lose their way."

"I see you have a pig in your pasture. Do hikers rent him, too?"

"That's Minette. No, she's not for rent. She would be quite worthless on the trail. I use her to find truffles."

"Oh, yes, I've heard of truffle pigs. Minette doesn't look like a truffle pig to me."

"What are truffle pigs supposed to look like?"

"I imagine they have ears that look like big, white flowers with ants crawling around in them."

"I think you've been on the trail too long, Madame. Minette is just a plain old pig with ordinary ears, as you can see, although they may have bugs in them. Some people use dogs, but I prefer pigs because they find truffles naturally. Dogs must be trained. Of course, pigs like to eat what they find, dogs don't."

"So how does Minette find truffles?"

"I bring her to a truffle patch and let her dig in the dirt under the oaks. Before she can eat any truffles she turns up, I snatch them away and give her a chocolate bar. At the end of the day, I give her a bottle of beer."

"You give Minette beer and chocolate!"

"No, no," said the farmer with a laugh, "even though chocolate and beer are much less expensive than truffles. I usually give her small bits of fruit and vegetables and drink the beer myself. Have you ever eaten truffles?"

"No. I've never had one."

"Ah, you wouldn't eat one. You only eat very thin slices such as in salads, meats, or sauces. They're a sort of mushroom. You must not be from this region."

"No," acknowledged Clare. "I'm not." She gazed at Minette another moment and then added, "People don't eat real truffles where I come from. They only eat chocolate truffles, which they find in expensive candy shops."

"I don't think Minette would be of much help in a candy shop. In fact, she might be the contrary."

When the farmer put the nail back into his mouth and turned to pick up his tools, Clare thought it was time to move on. She walked a little distance then turned to wave goodbye, but he had already moved to the next post and was again on his knees. Recalling the accordionist who played for the pleasure of hikers in the mountains above Conques, she would have gladly thrown a couple of euros into the farmer's hat if it had been lying nearby.

The Flour Mill Inn

The landscape had changed in response to the microclimate. Hills were blanketed with fields of dark green alfalfa soon ready to cut, and valleys flourished with corn, beans, and sunflowers still vivid as the day waned. At ease among crops of corn and beans, so common in Minnesota, she was inclined to sleep at the edge of a field that night, but wanting to be cautious, decided to look for a gite. When coming to a village, she spotted a Gite d'Etape sign with an arrow directing her to a peculiar house around which lay old-fashioned shafts, pulleys, and wheels. She walked up to the house and knocked on the door.

"Bonjour. Welcome to the Flour Mill Inn. Come in. My name is Frédérique, but just call me Fred. What's your name?"

"I'm Clare."

"Clare, do you have a reservation?"

"No, I don't. I was hoping you might have an extra place."

"Do you have a tent?"

"Yes, I do."

"Then we have a place for you. In fact, tenting here is free. You just pay for food, shower, and a washing machine if you want to wash clothes. Of course, the clothes lines and the air around them are also free."

"I'll take a tenting spot. Your gite looks like a mill."

"I hope so. It was a mill until we moved in and turned it into a gite. Actually, it was a broken down, old mill that hadn't been used since the 1960s. It's our summer home."

"You live elsewhere during the winter?"

"We have a winter home but not in France. We go to Gabon during the winter and teach in a high school. I teach French and my husband teaches math."

"Bonjour," said a man coming out of the kitchen. "My name is Phillipe. If you are staying the night, I assume you have a tent."

"Yes, I do."

"Good. I'll give you a tour of our facilities and show you a spot to pitch your tent. Put your sack and sticks on a chair and come along. Do you know it might rain tonight?"

"I'll manage. I've tented in rain before."

"You don't seem like the tourist type."

"I've been walking a few weeks."

"If you've been walking that long and you sleep in a tent, you aren't a tourist. I get a little brusque and crusty with the tourist type. They don't have a feel for the trail. Helping anyone who's carrying thirty pounds of baggage is very annoying."

Philippe led Clare to a long horse barn. Entering through a large double door at one end, they crossed a haymow packed with hiking gear, washing machines, and clothes lines, passed two bathrooms, then walked down a dimly lit passageway alongside a row of curtained, horse stalls. Converted into sleeping quarters for two, each stall had two beds, one on each side, and a non-functioning horse fountain attached to a feed bunk between them. Clare noted that despite the considered lack of elegance, everything was clean and orderly.

On the back side of the stable, the brook that had at one time powered the mill, still flowed. At the top of steps leading down to the water were a half-dozen pairs of rubber sandals for anyone who wanted to wade in the cool water after a day of walking. In keeping with the rusticity of the gite, six speckled brown chickens strutted about, scratching in the dirt, chasing slow moving bugs, and pecking at tan-shelled snails. Philippe said that one of the chickens had disappeared for a time, and he never expected to see her again, but on the tenth day she returned, fit as a fiddle. From then on she was known as the prodigal chicken, although he didn't know which one it was because they all looked alike. Philippe showed Clare a spot for her tent under a tree behind the stable, then walked with her back to the house to resume his job in the kitchen.

Dinner that evening consisted typically of an entrée, main dish, and dessert. It began with Philippe moving around the table, edging between the seated hikers to fill their glasses, one with white wine, the other with water. Fred followed, setting a small plate of shrimp covered with a thick white herb sauce before each guest. When they finished serving, host and hostess sat down, and everyone began to eat and talk.

Dinner was a convergence of hikers coming from east and west. Some had been on the trail for months and were coming back from Santiago. Others, less experienced, were going toward it. Two of those going west were Swiss women. The one sitting across from Clare introduced herself as Emilie. When Emilie said she worked for an American company in Geneva and was approaching retirement, Clare thought that walking the trail must be difficult at her age. But she revised that opinion when the other Swiss woman, who was sitting at the end of the table, introduced herself as Cécile, the mother of Emilie. Both women walked the same distance Clare had that day. Their only concession to age, other than walking a little slower, was to alternate carrying a single backpack.

Philippe's wit and the engaging mix of hikers created an evening amusing and diverting. He pointed out that unimagined things, good and bad, happen along the trail, and if one is on it long enough, one will surely come across something out of the ordinary.

"Have any of you heard of the Japanese ladies?" he asked. When no one responded, he continued, "For a few days every summer a group of young Japanese women stay at a gite west of here. On some days they dress up in traditional flowery kimonos with wide colorful sashes, put on makeup, and with fresh flowers in their hair, stroll through the village."

"How quixotic and strange," said a woman. "They must cause quite a stir."

"Yes, they do," replied Philippe. "The moment they step out of the gite, the owner alerts the mayor, who spreads the word around town. People in the streets stop to gaze at them, and traffic slows as they sashay about in their kimonos and thick white sandals."

The exoticism of the Japanese ladies prompted a woman coming from the West to ask, "Have any of you seen the cats?" When there was no response, she continued, "There is a town west of here known for its cats. I arrived late in the afternoon, ate dinner at a restaurant, then began looking for a few of these famous creatures. As luck would have it, I saw a couple of them lying lazily on window ledges, another peering impishly from a gutter high above the ground, another asleep on top of a post, and one sitting playfully in a niche in the wall. If I had continued looking, I would have found more, I'm sure, but the sun was going down and shadows were beginning to darken the neighborhoods."

"What is so unusual about cats hanging around town?" someone asked.

"It was eerie to see these cats," the storyteller continued. "There was a strange similarity about them. All were gray, and all ignored me as I passed. It was as though their color had faded with the diming light of day, and the endless curiosity of hikers had made them indifferent. Despite their blasé nature and lack of color, I am sure they will remain a spectacle and curiosity for years to come."

"They must have been very strange, indeed," said another hiker. "How can such passive, colorless cats be so interesting?"

"They were made of cement," replied the storyteller with a whimsical smile.

When the murmur of laughter subsided, another hiker said, "I think you made these cats as interesting as the Japanese ladies by your manner of telling the tale. I am going west and will stop to see these animals for myself."

While everyone was listening to the story of the cats, Fred returned to the kitchen and filled plates with the main course, a couscous and lamb tagine resting in a spicy, brown sauce. When the plates were ready, she brought them two by two from the kitchen, setting one before each guest, and Philippe made a second tour of the table, this time with a Bordeaux red.

As the main course began, a younger man began an amusing story about a sheepherder and a bird. "Along the trail high in the Pyrenees," he said, "I met a sheepherder who explained how he got tricked by a bird."

"This too seems be an odd tale. I can't imagine how a sheepherder could be tricked by a bird," commented a hiker. "It must have been a mockingbird."

"I will explain. When bringing his sheep into the mountains for the summer, the herder used dogs to move the herd forward. To direct sheep in one direction or another he whistled signals to the dogs telling them to turn the herd right, left, or continue straight ahead. One day as the herd was moving tranquilly forward, the dogs suddenly turned the sheep to the left and led them off in an odd direction. The herder was surprised and confused at first but managed to get the herd back on course. This unexpected change of direction occurred again that afternoon, and it wasn't until the end of the day that he discovered how this happened. During the evening when the dogs were resting and the sheep still, he heard an imitation of his own whistle coming from the trees and realized that a bird had mimicked his signals to the dogs."

"That was a cheeky bird," said a hiker. "I imagine him sitting in a tree laughing at the herder as the sheep were running off."

This narrative encouraged a man coming from the West to tell his story. "I have a tale about a different kind of bird, I think less amusing but just as interesting. If you are going west, you will surely see vultures circling overhead as you climb the Pyrenees. Sometimes these big birds find dead sheep and eat them. I stopped to talk to a herder who said that each of his sheep was insured, and if one is killed by wolves or falls off a cliff, he takes the numbered tag from the ear of the animal and sends it to the government to be reimbursed. The problem with vultures is that they sometimes eat the tag along with the sheep, and there is no record of the animal's death."

"I'm glad I'm not wearing earrings," joked a woman.

"If you see vultures circling above, don't worry about them. They won't eat you or your earrings, unless, of course, you've been killed by wolves or fallen off a cliff."

The peculiar image of vultures eating animal tags and women's earrings provoked pensive murmurs and quiet chuckles that encouraged a young woman to recount a story that was almost as bizarre. "I was staying at a gite whose owner said he had seen a camel and goat trot past, each with a load of camping equipment on its back. When I expressed a bit of skepticism by asking him what he had been smoking that day, he protested loudly, saying that other gite owners farther along the trail must also have seen these same animals, and I should just ask them. Have any of you seen a camel and goat along the trail?"

That question created a buzz of laughter. When it died down a little, a young man replied, "No, I haven't seen a camel or a goat yet, but perhaps I will." When he added, "Does anyone have a box of matches to spare?" the laughter reignited.

By now diners had fallen under the spell of these accounts and imagined coming across something odd along the trail. This romanticism began to diminish though when the camel and goat story reminded a veteran hiker of his experience with corrida bulls.

"I am coming back from Santiago," he said. "Not long after crossing the border into France, I took a shortcut that led me between two pastures of fighting bulls."

'I didn't realize France had bullfighting," interrupted a hiker.

"Yes, there is bullfighting in France, and you will see arenas southwest of here. Bullfighting has been a tradition in that region for centuries even though it's illegal in the rest of the country."

"That is such an awful sport," someone else added. "Against picadors and matadors, bulls have no chance. Their slaughter is a spectacle for bloodthirsty audiences. I don't understand how people can watch."

"I remember going to a bullfight in a small arena in Spain," said another hiker. "The weather was bad, and everyone brought umbrellas. About the time the corrida started, it began to rain. We all put up our umbrellas, which made viewing the spectacle almost impossible, and the matador was as inexperienced as he was wet. The whole thing was an ugly disaster."

"I bet it's good for the tourism industry," a pragmatic hiker pointed out.

The storyteller resumed his narrative. "As I was walking between the two pastures, the animals eyed me suspiciously, but since they were on the other side of the fence, I figured I had nothing to worry about. A little farther on, however, as I was daydreaming, I almost walked into two bulls that had jumped the fence. They were standing on the trail with heads down, horns leveled, and eyes fixed on me. Since there was no way around them, I slowly backed away until coming to a small tree, which at that time seemed no larger than a medium-size bush. I crouched behind this tree until they finally lost interest and ambled away."

When the hiker ended his story with "that was the first time I was pleased to see the back end of a bull," the guests again broke into laughter, this time restrained by a bit of aversion.

After the tagine had been eaten and stories came to an end, Philippe circled the table, offering more wine. Fred gathered up the empty dishes, brought them to the kitchen, and returned with a large platter of pineapple triangles and orange roundels sprinkled with sugar and kirsch. She set the platter in the middle of the table for everyone to admire then handed a spatula to the nearest guest.

As hikers filled their plates with the sweet dessert, a new conversation began. The romanticism of the trail diminished with the telling of the bull story and extinguished altogether when Philippe said, "As hikers you probably wouldn't know that some villages have too many gites, and there are conflicts among the owners. Luckily, that isn't a problem here."

"The trail is big business. I assume there would be competition," responded the pragmatic hiker.

"There is also conflict between Gite owners, who want to attract hikers, and residents who do not like strangers coming into their villages. There is a man west of here who moves GR 65 signs. More than one hiker has had to retrace steps and consult his map a second and third time to find the trail. I don't think this man owns a gite," said Phillipe with a sardonic smile.

"The trail also has its degenerates," added a hiker. "I've heard of a pervert who exposes himself to single women on the trail."

“He probably doesn’t own a gite either,” responded Philippe, starting cascade of snickering and laughter.

“I would like to say, though, that most people living along the trail, especially those who have taken it themselves, appreciate hikers,” said a man who was returning from the west. “When I went through a village in Spain, I stopped at a cafe to get something to eat and watch a football match. At break time I got up from my table and went to the toilet. When I came back, my walking sticks were gone. I rushed up to the bar and asked the barman if he had seen someone take them, but he was busy serving drinks and hadn’t noticed anything, and the patrons were focused on the match. I went back to my table, irritated as hell. While I sat there imagining my climb into the Pyrenees without sticks, a hiker came over to me saying he had been to Santiago. Now almost home, he offered me his.”

With that final story, dinner ended on a positive note. But there was one more thing to come, a digestive to finish the convivial evening. When hikers sat down to eat, they noticed a long plank suspended a couple of feet above the table with many little bottles of colored liquids standing on it in two long rows. There were comments about this interesting contraption, and everyone assumed it was merely an odd part of the decor. But as guests prepared to leave the table, the plank suddenly dropped to within inches of cups and glasses. Everyone gasped. Philippe had released a pulley which allowed the plank to come down. The purpose of this ingenious system was to offer an after-dinner drink and let everyone know the dining room was closing. Explaining he once dropped the plank on his own eyeglasses, he set a shot glass in front of each guest and invited them to sample the liquors before them. Their choices were ginger, pear, plum, mint, mango, and peach.

It rained lightly during the night, but asleep under the tree near the wall of the stable, Clare hardly noticed. The next morning, she woke early, showered, packed her equipment, and went to the mill house for breakfast. Bread, butter, jam, yogurt, hot chocolate, coffee, and fruit were displayed neatly at one end of the table. Fred and Philippe sat casually at the other end, drinking coffee, and discussing chores of the day.

"Bonjour," said Clare. "You start early."

"We try to get up with the chickens," said Philippe.

"Bonjour, Clare," Fred replied. "Help yourself. There's no tea. We forgot to buy tea."

"Maybe you would like a drink. I can always lower the plank," added Philippe.

"Oh, no thank you. I think I will just have coffee with my breakfast. I don't want to fall off the trail and get eaten by vultures."

Clare finished breakfast as other guests began drifting in, and before Fred and Philippe got caught up in serving them, she paid her bill and asked to have her créanciale signed. When Philippe handed it back to her, she thanked her hosts for the pleasant stay, said goodbye to them and the hikers at the table, and left.

Walking at a vigorous, upbeat pace, she made her way into the countryside. With the sun low and the morning cool and damp, she noticed spider webs at the edge of the trail. Covered with a delicate crystalline condensation, the webs sparkled against the dark background of wet vegetation and morning shadows. Some looked like silver diaphanous blankets descending from the tops of pasture fences to the undergrowth below, and many had a characteristic double zigzag strand, the hallmark of a certain type of spider, running from center to outer edge. She stopped now and then to admire the work of these natural weavers.

As the morning progressed, the condensation dried away and the webs disappeared in the sunlight. Farther down the trail she came to a stand of bamboo, and beyond the bamboo she crossed an orchard of kiwi and came to a large field of ripening cantaloupe. At the edge of this field stood a rickety wooden table, gray and cracked with age, holding a half-dozen melons and a rusty, red metal box upon which was stamped the words Children's Charity. Next to the box stood a melons-for-sale sign. Enticed by the fruity aroma drifting across the field, she stopped at the table, picked melons up one by one and put them to her nose. When satisfied with a certain one, she fished a couple of euros out of her pocket and dropped them into the box. Sitting on the soft ground amongst weeds and vines, she cut the melon in two, set one half on her pack, and began eating the other. Savoring every spoonful, she ate slowly.

The tranquility of the field brought her back to the Flour Mill Inn. It was as though old friends had gathered there for an evening. She had been enchanted by the stories and anecdotes of her fellow hikers and amused by Phillippe and his way of closing the dining room. At the beginning of her walk, she had stopped at a gite named "l'Abri" to admire a garden and watch a dog, and farther down the trail she learned that "abri" meant a place of shelter and refuge. When starting from Le Puy, she had little intention of staying in gites, but along the way this quaint fusion of restaurant and home, such as the Flour Mill Inn, had become a respite and shelter.

This need for shelter was due to the healer, now lurking persistently in her mind, sometimes in the background, sometimes at the fore. She could not imagine him sitting at the table with other hikers at the Flour Mill Inn. Feeling ill at ease and out of place, he would be sullen and graceless. And she wondered how he would respond to the little table of fruit and generosity next to which she sat. Without the constraint of others nearby, would he eat a melon, take the few coins lying in the money box and walk off? Or would he smash the melons and table and take the money, trying to satisfy a deep antisocial rage?

She finished the half melon, set the empty rind on the ground, and picked up the other half. As she scraped seeds from this part, she pondered the healer's character from a different perspective, as though it were the other half of the melon. Not entirely convinced he was as evil as she sometimes imagined, she thought that perhaps the scene of his stealing and smashing was only a farfetched invention of fear, and she had no real reason to suspect him of theft or violence. Maybe he was just lewd and uncouth like the two potheads on the cafe patio.

When she had eaten the second half of the melon, she threw the rinds into the vines and put thoughts of the healer aside. She wiped the blade of the knife on a broad leaf, slipped it into her backpack, and returned to the trail. Her sense of environment having been intensified by the aroma of the patch and the taste of melon, she slowed her pace to absorb the fruitfulness of the countryside.

A few miles beyond the melon patch she came across two hikers making their way at a pace even slower than hers. A teenage boy on one knee was taking photos of something in the grass, while a woman stood nearby on the trail apparently waiting for him. When Clare arrived, she stopped to talk and discovered the woman was the boy's mother and his passion was taking photos of insects. Standing side by side looking over the little expanse of low vegetation, the two women watched the boy move his camera back and forth, tracking an insect with the concentration of a big game hunter. The intensity with which he worked reminded Clare first of the Parisian woman who had taken photos of stones in the wall of the church, and then, incongruously, of the pot smokers, whose indolence at the cafe contrasted so sharply with the passion of the boy. After watching the young photographer for a few moments, she picked up her pack, said goodbye to the mother, and moved on.

A half-hour later she stopped to rest. Sitting on a rock along the trail, she pulled out her water bottle, and while taking a drink, noticed a green, stick-like insect as large as her hand swaying back and forth on the vegetation between her boots. Almost imperceptible, it was feasting on a leafy blade of grass, chewing the edges into jagged, irregular patterns. Thinking this creature would be a prime subject for the young photographer and assuming the boy and his mother were coming her way, she waited. When they arrived, she hailed them and pointing to her feet, suggested he take photos. It took the boy several moments to discern the insect, even with his trained eye, but when he finally did, she cautiously retracted her feet and pivoted away. He then went to work, aiming his camera and snapping photos. While he worked, she said goodbye to the mother a second time, and turned to the trail, imagining the photographic record the boy would have to show his science class when returning to high school in the fall.

At noon she came to a village and stopped for lunch.

"What would you like?" asked the waiter.

"What do you put on your sandwiches?"

"Sliced cheese, salami, bacon, tomatoes, lettuce, and a hardboiled egg with mayonnaise or mustard are the usual items."

"I'll have a sandwich with everything on it except bacon and mayonnaise, and an Orangina."

When the waiter returned with her order, Clare said, "I hope you don't mind my muddy boots."

"Oh, no, muddy floors are part of the job. Hikers often come into the restaurant with dirty boots after rain. The worst time is the spring."

She picked up the sandwich and began to eat, but had taken only a few bites when through the window she saw the two Swiss women crossing the intersection a little beyond the cafe. It was Cécile's turn to carry the backpack, and Clare noticed that even with extra weight on her shoulders, the old woman moved steadily forward, aided only by a pair of walking sticks. Emilie stood just beyond the curb looking both ways for traffic. Realizing she was being passed by an eighty-year-old, Clare hoped that in fifty years she would be able to move as well as Cécile.

On the way out of the village after lunch she passed a school in front of which stood a brick pedestal with a plaque attached to it. Stopping to read the inscription on the plaque, she was surprised to see that the school was dedicated to the Inuits of Quebec in recognition of hospitality given to French voyagers who traded with them in the eighteenth century. Clifford Moar, chief of the Inuits at the time of the dedication, came to receive expressions of gratitude and give a speech.

Farther down the trail she passed houses that had holes in their walls just under the eaves. In and out of these holes flew swallows and pigeons, making her wonder why people constructed homes so accommodating to birds. A little farther on she came to a cement structure that reminded her of the shepherd's hut she had slept in. Standing on four tall, stone pillars, it had no steps or visible entry for humans, and its walls, like those of the houses she had just passed, were pierced with holes through which birds continually entered and left.

As she stood looking at this strange structure, Cécile and Emilie came up the trail.

"Bonjour, Mademoiselle," greeted Cécile. "The trail hasn't been too muddy for you?"

"Bonjour, Mesdames. It's not as difficult as it was this morning. And for you?"

"We manage despite the weather," said Emilie.

"Do you know what this strange building is?" asked Clare.

"I have no idea, but I'm sure some resident along the trail will tell us if we ask," said Cécile.

"Do you mind if I walk with you for a while?" asked Clare.

"You may walk with us, but you might get impatient. Eighty-two-year-olds don't walk fast, you know," responded Cécile.

"You are in remarkable condition."

"Living in the mountains, I can hardly leave the house without either climbing or descending, though now it seems I do more climbing."

"Why are you taking this trail when there are so many beautiful places to walk in Switzerland?"

"We just wanted to see different country and meet different people," said Emilie.

"Are you walking to Santiago?"

"No. A month is all the time I have, although mother has been talking about walking all the way."

"Yes, I would like to keep going," responded Cécile.

"You want to worship at the shrine?" asked Clare.

"Yes, I do, but I want to arrive by walking. For me walking is a way into the future. I have many wonderful memories, but since I can't return to the past and relive those moments, I want to keep moving forward. When I stop moving, I will have plenty of time in eternity to muse and brood about the past."

Clare walked with Cécile and Emilie until they arrived at a hamlet where the Swiss women decided to stop and rest. Clare, who was neither tired nor hungry, said she would continue.

"It's been a pleasure walking with you," said Emilie.

"Perhaps we'll meet again farther down the trail," added her mother.

"I look forward to that," said Clare, charmed by Cécile's spirit. She then bade mother and daughter farewell and turned to leave.

How strong Cécile is, thought Clare, as she walked away from the women. She is not afraid of life or death and insists on walking to the end. This need to keep moving made Clare wonder if that was why she herself was so intent on biking and hiking. Was she, like Cécile, compelled by notions of time and eternity to keep going forward?

It seemed to Clare that Cécile imagined being transported into a kind of poetic eternity after death, leaving life on earth to meditate elsewhere. Clare had heard stories about people assuming they would reunite with loved ones after death. Comforting ideas like this implied that life in some form or other continued after death. But as much as she admired Cécile, she could not agree with her imaginative conception of eternity, although she agreed with her that death was not the end. Clare thought of eternity in terms of science and fundamental laws, not in terms of mythology and poetry. When she died, she and her accomplishments would be remembered for a time and then fade away as her effect on people dwindled. But her atoms would last as long as the earth existed. At death she would return to the soil, and the atoms and molecules of her body would be recycled into different earthly elements in a natural and eternal process of movement and renewal.

Her notion of movement and eternity was not founded on imaginative thinking but on Lavoisier's eighteenth century principle of conservation, which hypothesized that mass is neither created nor destroyed, only reorganized, and transformed. This idea of transformation was comforting because there was neither heaven nor hell to which people were sent depending on evaluation of their character, and it reduced the great prophets and saints to mere historical figures, some good, some bad.

The idea of transformation made her think about her own death and led her to imagine a hive of honey bees standing at the edge of a small, country cemetery where she is buried. As her body, along with its wooden coffin disintegrates, her atoms and molecules become part of the soil that nourishes the flowers around the gravestones. The flowers in turn provide life-giving energy for a hive, and the hive contributes to this cycle when its occupants die to become part of the soil. This concept of recycling was more interesting and attractive to Clare than the idea of sitting around for eternity musing and brooding about one's earthly life if one were good or writhing with regret in the flames of hell if one were bad.

She stopped at a village cafe for an early dinner. While waiting on the patio for her order, she noticed a publicity poster taped to the window next to her shoulder. It listed regional summer events including a farm festival celebrating livestock and work animals, a disco ball, a tractor-pulling contest, a monster tractor show, and Montgolfier rides. The region seemed to pulsate with summer fairs and festivities.

Thinking about the old-fashioned threshing bees and county fairs in rural Minnesota, she was surprised to see Martin coming up the road. Sticks in hand and a little thinner, he was moving at his steady, durable pace. She hailed him from her table, this time in a more pleasant manner than she had in the foggy hills farther east. He crossed the road, set his pack on the ground, and dropped into the chair across from her.

"Well, we meet again. I caught up with you," he said. "You must have slowed down."

"I may have slowed a little. My pace seems to respond more to the environment."

As though they had chatted just that morning, Martin began by asking, "So, you've had time to think. What have you been thinking?"

"Nothing profound, just commonplace thoughts about life, death, and countryside."

"I've found a kind of ordinariness in the trail," said Martin. "By now I've stayed in a lot of gites and met hikers of all sorts. I feel as though I am part of a fluid, moving band.

"I suppose you've been wrestling with life's great issues?"

"Well, I wouldn't say I've been wrestling with anything that important, but I've been thinking, as I already told you, about what I am going to do when I return home. It's been helpful to meet people along the way who motivate me to do something worthwhile."

"And walking to a great religious shrine has had an effect on you?"

"Yes, it has, but not how you might think. I've come to realize that the shrine, the architecture, and all the icons along the trail are an elegant response to things unknown and inexplicable."

"What has the unknown and inexplicable to do with finding a retirement activity?"

"Remember when we met? We stopped at a chapel and talked about Roman architecture and the four Gospel writers. Those paintings, the chapel, and all the icons we've seen along the way respond to a certain human instinct."

"What instinct is that?"

"Religions develop out of fear of the unknown present and future, and I think this fear is the underlying stimulus for the art and architecture along the trail."

"How's that?"

"Have you ever seen old maps of the ancient world? Explorers, practical and realistic, drew maps of where they had been, but cartographers, who stayed home at their tables and easels to refine these maps, added frightening images of creatures living in places just beyond what had been explored."

"But this imagery disappeared as explorers continued to move across the planet. Every bit of the Earth has now been explored and there are no more monsters."

"Fearful imagery may have disappeared from maps, but much in our existence is still unknown, and fear remains. This fear, for example, led to a great, comforting mythology called Christianity, which provided a savior, endless life, and eternal happiness for the loyal and committed."

"So, religions of all kinds provide psychological comfort and protection for believers."

"Yes, they do. The desire to be religious is a powerful force, and I think evolution and genetics play a role in the development of this force."

"First you talk about mapmaking and now genetics and evolution. I'm getting lost. What do genetics and evolution have to do with religion?"

"Human beings are genetically programed to live in groups for protection, just like animals. Yaks form tight circles and put their horns down when threatened by hungry wolves on the Arctic tundra. Humans are much advanced in medicine, communication, and space exploration, but socially they have hardly evolved beyond yaks and wolves. With that group mentality, we are still in the tribal stage of evolution."

"Grouping is needed for survival. How could we exist without groups?"

"Tribalism is the result of people fearing others who are not like themselves, and as people with different cultural or genetic characteristics come together, fear increases, creating potential for aggression and violence. As you probably know, an eye for an eye and a tooth for a tooth is a common expression in Christianity. Human existence has not yet been fully explored and understood. We need to find a higher way of thinking."

"I take it you weren't planning to become a priest or pastor when returning to Geneva."

"In Geneva there are organizations for labor, migration, human rights, refugees, health, climate, and on and on, dozens and dozens. Their common goal is to cross barriers, whether religious, political, or racial, to help whoever needs help. Living among people who work for these organizations and meeting people on the trail like them have had an influence on me. They make me want to do something useful, tangible, governed by ethics and logic, not by fear of differences and the unknown. The other day I met a gite owner who has since become my inspiration, a remarkable woman."

"She must have been something special."

"Things don't always work out as planned and sometimes that's good. Usually I don't bother with reservations, but I knew the town I planned to stay in would be packed with tourists and hikers, so I reserved a bed at a gite. As I sat on the steps of the gite waiting for the door to be opened, a tall British girl dropped her pack, sat down next to me, and asked if I knew of a place to stay.

"I thought first of the gite where I planned to stay but remembered my reservation had brought it to full capacity for the night. I noticed a gite sign on a house almost directly across the street, so I suggested going there to inquire. She asked me to guard her stuff, went across the street, and tapped on the door. A few minutes later she came out followed by an old lady close on her heels who was grumbling loudly about something. Looking frustrated and a little desperate, the Brit scurried back to where I sat and said she did not want to stay there.

"About the time the Brit returned to the steps, the door of my gite opened. I suggested she follow me in and take a chance on finding a room there. Ironically, I provided her with a place to stay. When I spoke to the owner, who was sitting at a desk in the entry hall, he said he did not live in the house but down the street. I didn't think that living somewhere else was unusual, but when he said he began serving breakfast at seven a.m. I decided to find another gite since I wanted to be on the trail by that time, and the Brit took my place.

"Now I had her problem, where to go. I walked across the street and rang the bell, expecting to face a tiger. The same old lady, straight and stern, came to the door and let me in. When I explained my situation, she showed me a room with two king size beds and a balcony in the back which overlooked a beautiful, well-tended garden. The shower and toilet were outside on the balcony but that didn't matter to me even though the nights got chilly. I took the room, and she introduced herself as Justa.

"I was curious about why she did not accept the Brit but dared not ask. Later she told me the girl was looking for a place to pitch her tent. Justa did not want anyone sleeping in her garden, and thinking the Brit's request was impertinent, escorted her out. At dinner I learned my hostess was a very independent Basque widow, whose guiding principle was that hard work and attention to others are the essence of life. She said all four of her children had good jobs because they knew how to work hard, and two of them worked in Geneva for humanitarian organizations. Of course, her children learned much of their attitude from their mother. Throughout the evening she accommodated and pampered hikers as though they were guests in an opulent nineteenth century hotel. Her attention was almost constraining. When I came down at six a. m. breakfast was on the table, and she was standing by the kitchen counter ready to serve. As I left her at the door that morning, I decided on my future.

"About twenty percent of Switzerland's population are immigrants. Many come from eastern Europe and Syria, a few from Africa. I remember seeing an improvised feeding station for newly arrived immigrants on a street in Geneva. Every day random volunteers drove up with food to distribute from a makeshift stand on a sidewalk, and hungry, ragged people appeared from nowhere. Children pulled on the sleeves of volunteers begging for cookies and candy, older immigrants waited expectantly. It was both a sad and happy scene. With the change of climate there will be a great displacement of people, and more and more immigrants will arrive. I'm going to get involved, not at a political or administrative level, but at street level. I'm going to start by finding a building to distribute food. Then I will look for a place to house immigrants."

As Martin was describing his project, a waiter came with Clare's order. She invited Martin to stay and share food with her, but he looked at his watch and said he needed to reach the next town before nightfall.

Before he left, she had one last question. "Why doesn't the Swiss government simply open vacant buildings for these people?"

"It has," he replied, "but the government does not want the country to become a magnet for immigrants, so it limits what it provides for those who arrive."

Shouldering his pack, Martin said, "The trail has power to change people if they are open to it. When I began, I had no thoughts of working with immigrants, but now it seems like the right thing to do. They need food, clothing, shelter, and medical attention." He then shook Clare's hand, said goodbye, and returned to the trail.

Considering Martin's idealistic nature, Clare was not surprised at his plan. It was his expression of how he felt about people. It seemed that if hikers were changed by the trail, it was because they were receptive to the humanity living and flowing along the way and not because of the shrines and icons they encountered. Sébastien started his gite to support walkers because he had hiked the trail and was thankful. And the history professor, who had given her the sky map, walked the trail as a sign of protest against the wicked nuns and priest in the Spanish internment camp. But she was not so naïve to think that everyone taking the trail was receptive to this spirit. At the Flour Mill Inn Phillipe called the unaffected ones tourists because they were preoccupied with themselves and unchanged by their walk.

Wondering if she would ever meet Martin again, Clare glanced at the vacant chair and stared indifferently across the landscape. She picked at her food for a few moments, then pushing plate and silverware aside, reached into her backpack for the sky map. Unfolding it across the table, she scanned the skies searching for Ursa Major and Ursa Minor, and when finding them, began tracing constellations with her finger and naming them as she moved from one constellation to the next. When confident she could locate at least a few in the sky that night, she folded the map and finished eating.

Not yet ready to start walking, she pulled out *Zen and the Art of Motorcycle Maintenance* and lay it unopened on the table. Studying the constellations and finding them in the sky required perception. Understanding philosophy was a matter of comprehension. Neither was easy. By now she realized the peg upon which Pirsig hung his philosophy was that a motorcyclist, who knew how to maintain his machine, was riding with a couple, who did not. Using that simple framework, he had made his way into a philosophical argument about how objective and subjective thinking were needed to achieve quality, or, as she understood it, truth.

Having read only a part of the book and not yet clear about how to achieve quality, she studied the photos on the cover, hoping to find meaning there. At the top was a photo of a large, green, mechanical bearing with three of its steel balls partially exposed. She knew that bearings had a purpose on the motorcycle, but their metallic hardness and geometric form scarcely interested her. At the bottom was a photo of riders on motorcycles traveling across flat grassland that reminded her of the Dakotas. She was drawn to this photo because it suggested adventure and freedom on western roads. When she studied the two photos together, the relationship between traveling and bearings was obvious. Motorcycles don't move without bearings. But she saw no clue about how to achieve quality in that link.

Unable to find anything of greater significance in the relationship of the two photos, she opened the book and browsed among its pages. When nothing new came to her, she closed it and returned the cover. While studying the photos a second time, she changed her point of view and thought of herself in relation to the images. When she did this, she began to see a metaphor emerge from the relationship. By comparing her reaction to the invented object in the top photo with her reaction to the adventurous ride in the bottom one, she began to see how rationalism gives riders the means to maintain their machines and stay on the road, while subjectivism, the spiritual and romantic attraction of the road, urges them to ride and explore. This metaphor, as she now understood it, showed how both rationalism and subjectivism together were needed to find quality.

Satisfied with her interpretation of the need for both rationalism and subjectivism in the search for quality, she turned to the word Zen. She had not finished reading what Pirsig had to say about Zen, but when asking herself what Zen had to do with this search, she concluded that since pure logic was inadequate and subjective knowledge could not be relied upon, Zen was required as the discipline to blend the logic of rationalism with the emotion of subjectivism.

Satisfied with her interpretation of Pirsig's metaphor, whether simplistic or perceptive, she put the book into her backpack, slipped the sky map in next to it, and went to the counter to pay her bill. As the cashier was handing her change, she asked about the homes with holes in them and the house standing on pillars. He replied that during the

Middle Ages there were few domestic animals but many gardens and tiny farms in the region. People constructed homes with holes for bird nests because they needed food for the table and fertilizer for the garden. The richest farmers constructed large dwellings on stands that could hold dozens of nests and many birds.

An Atomic Walk into Eternity

She descended the long eastern slope of a valley, crossed the flat bottom, and began ascending the steeper western side. Seeing a small grove of trees near the crest to the left, she decided to camp there for the night, wanting to observe the stars. As the sun neared the horizon, she mounted the low wall along the trail, dropped into the harvested wheatfield on the other side, and walked across the stubble up to the trees. From there she could see the valley below and the sky above.

By the time she put the tent up and stashed her equipment, the grove had darkened, and the sky had begun to awaken with the faint light of celestial bodies. Putting on her jacket to keep mosquitoes at bay, she sat against the trunk of a fallen tree, and peered into the heavens. Slowly, one by one, or perhaps millions by millions, stars competing with the moon to be noticed appeared, and as the evening lengthened, constellations, discreetly defining themselves, emerged among them. She did not understand how constellations formed but knew that what kept them from disintegrating was the powerful force of gravity. This constancy of form was reassuring and comforting, and seeing constellations emerge from the sky in the same place night after night was like visiting a familiar childhood haunt.

Scanning the heavens and contemplating the effects of gravity brought her back to Pirsig. As she understood him, Pirsig defined quality as insight into the fundamental nature of man and universe, and this insight created an awareness that resisted the tribalism of racism, religion, and nationalism. Martin had said that mankind needed to evolve beyond tribalism to a higher way of thinking, and she saw Pirsig's search for quality as a way to do that. But achieving the required balance of subjectivity and objectivity is not easy. She had studied the cover of Pirsig's book, indifferent to the photo of the bearings but stirred by the photo of the cyclists riding across the prairie. She remembered standing in the flowery meadow listening to the plaintive call of the cuckoo and thinking of it as a tragic victim. And she thought of Sal in *On the Road,* whose self-indulgent trip from the East Coast to San Francisco was a fruitless, mystical search. The photo on the cover, the poignant bird call, and the excesses of Sal made her realize that emotion and subjectivity were inadequate in the search for quality.

She lowered her eyes and gazed at the wheat stubble undulating across the valley in a gently rising night breeze. Fatigued by the poetic complexity of Pirsig's book and mesmerized by the moving stubble in the dwindling twilight, she imagined seeing the ghostly forms of two old men standing in the field below. Dressed in ancient attire, they stood close together with their backs to her, looking upward, talking animatedly. She watched them for many moments wondering who they were. Finally, when one pointed skyward and the other followed his imaginary line of sight into the heavens, she recognized them. They were the familiar Copernicus and Galileo, and she understood why they were in the field. Inspired by the stars and guided by the logic of science, they were seekers of quality and truth, and she knew they would have well understood Pirsig's metaphor of the cycle ride illustrating the co-dependence of objective mechanics and subjective exploration.

The astronomers stayed for a time then disappeared into the night, but neither her gaze nor imagination shifted away from the valley. Where the two men had been standing, she now saw slabs of white limestone lying in the stubble and illuminated by the light of the moon. Stones like these had long been a curse to farmers, but she was not thinking of their struggle with them at this moment. Rather she was imagining the slabs to be soldiers dead on the prairie of Compostelle. They could have been Romans and tribesmen from the first century or Christians and Moors from the ninth. Whoever they were, they had joined the mythical brotherhood of the dead and become equal and passive.

She pondered the lives and deaths of these imaginary soldiers, then was propelled centuries forward to the time when she herself had arrived at Compostelle. Standing on the prairie where the soldier in the Roman camp had observed the stars and created his poem, she was looking at the cathedral, thinking about the relics of James and of all the trappings and rituals within that testified to his saintliness and imaginary leadership in war against the Moors. To her, the cathedral was as irrational as the two battles fought centuries apart on the prairie surrounding it. When the image of the cathedral faded away, she returned to the present. James, however, continued lingering in her mind, and while he was there, she discovered a similarity between him and the shimmering, white slabs. His bones were as inert as the stones that lay in the stubble, and neither the bones nor the stones gave encouragement or cheer.

Wanting to push the gloom of war and religion out of mind, she left the fallen tree and went to the tent to retrieve her pillow, sleeping bag, and mattress. Laying them in the stubble, she slid into the bag and began to survey the sky on her back. The first star she found was Polaris, the familiar North Star. From Polaris she followed an imaginary line to Delta, then to the next star and the next, until completing the handle and bowl that formed the Big Dipper. With the success of finding a familiar constellation, her patience increased, her perception adjusted, and she moved to a different part of the sky to look for the summer triangle of Vega, Lyra and a third star, whose name she could not remember.

To human beings looking up from Earth, stars seem to be constant and fixed. Sailors have guided their ships by them for millennia, first walkers were heartened by the sun's inevitable morning rise, and the Roman soldier poet found peace and encouragement in the constellations. But she knew these configurations would not last forever. In a million light years of travel, an instant in eternity, stars would assume new positions, and new constellations held together by the force of gravity would form. She imagined herself to be one of these celestial pilgrims, who connects with other pilgrims in the heavens for a cosmic moment to form a new constellation then moves on. This movement, she thought, was the celestial version of the corresponding forming and reforming of atoms and molecules on Earth, and it was this movement and change that gave eternal life to the heavens.

She wanted to sleep in the light of the dome that night but since mosquitoes had begun attacking in full force, decided to withdraw. Shaking the dirt and bugs from the mattress, she threw it along with the pillow, sleeping bag, and knife into the tent, and crawled in. Before sliding into the bag, she opened the knife, and lay it to the side in a gesture that brought the healer to mind. Even on this peaceful night under the stars, intuition whispered in her ear that he was not a good man. It told her that he was like a comet wheeling freely amongst the stars as though he were unaffected by the force of gravity. She slid into the bag and reached down to touch the knife in a ritual that turned it from mundane tool of day into weapon of night.

Drifting to sleep, she thought of Terry Fox, fearless and optimistic, and of the first walkers, naive and pure. She then recalled a story that Cécile had recounted at the Flour Mill Inn. "I remember going to a funeral of an old friend," she said. “The custom as one entered the church was to light a candle, place it next to other burning candles on a small table, and pray silently for the departed. Just before the funeral began, a family with a young daughter entered. When the father lit a candle and placed it on the table, the child began singing ‘Happy Birthday’ in an earnest and clear voice.” Cécile finished by saying, “I am sure God blessed this child for her sincerity.” To Clare, Cécile’s story was a parable of young and old, of birth and death, of stars repositioning to make new constellations, and of atoms forming and reforming to make new molecules and elements on Earth for eternity. She then fell into a serene slumber.

The healer sat on a rock in a clump of trees on the east side of the valley. He had watched her cross the stubble field, set up her tent on the crest, and sit against the tree. Now it was too dark to see her, but that didn’t make any difference. At the right time he would cross the valley and climb to her camp. He had fantasized about this moment since first touching her and sliding his hands up and down her legs, and while sitting behind her at the Club House Café, close enough to smell her hair and touch her arm, he had decided to act. He had had other women, but somehow this was the one he wanted, perhaps because she had rejected him. He would wait well into the night, then approach.

Hearing the tent zipper whizz open, Clare snapped awake but had no time to react. “I have a knife,” said the healer, “lie still.” He slid his left hand up and down the bag and felt the curves of her body. With a knee across her legs and his left hand on her chest, he pulled the zipper down and opened the sleeping bag. Stunned by his entry, she lay still and silent, but not frightened. The time to fight the wolf had arrived.

He pushed her shirt up and felt her breasts. Fearless, she waited. When he slipped his hand down into her panty, she slid her right arm down toward the knife. He unzipped his jeans and lay on top of her, his wine- reeking breath filling her nostrils. As he entered her, she grasped the knife. When he began to thrust, she extended her arm away from his body and drove the weapon into his side. In the midst of ecstasy, he felt a prick of pain. What could that have been? Was it part of his pleasure?

Just as he reached his peak, he felt it again, but this time a brutal pain between the ribs of his back. He knew now that something was wrong. Angered by pain, he arched backward, raised his arm, and slammed his knife into her chest. This gesture, however, left him exposed. He felt a third explosion of pain, and suddenly the tent became a prison. With all his force he pushed himself up and toppled backward out of the tent. Rolling onto his stomach, he crabbed a few yards into the stubble and stopped to rest. He had just enough strength to raise his head and look up at the gigantic starry dome. His head then lowered into the stubble, the sky went dark, and the constellations disappeared. Blood ran from his body and soon would begin dripping to the ground, seeping into the dirt. His molecules and atoms would be taken in through the roots of plants, honey bees would visit nearby flowers, and the recycling process begun. His long atomic walk into eternity had started.

Clare knew she could not stay in the tent. She had to get to the trail. She pulled up her panties, but unable to find her shorts, took her jacket and pillow and dragged herself out of the tent. Skirting the inert body of the healer, she lurched down the hill to the rock wall, leaving a slash of blood on the dry, gray moss and white stone as she climbed over and fell to the ground on the other side. Crawling to the trail's edge, she lay in the grass, covered herself with the jacket and tucked the blue, tubular pillow under her head. She would sleep until the constellations completed their arc across the sky and daylight came to extinguish the moon. Then in the morning, hikers, as they naturally did, would find her and gather round to help, and she would be lifted up, dusted off, and sent on her way.

With the rising of the next day's sun, hikers crawled out of tents or left gites to begin the day's walk. Among them was a piano teacher. He noticed her legs first. The one on the ground continued straight down from the body, the other extended forward but reversed direction at the knee and came back at an angle. She looked as though she were walking. He noticed a flowered panty just visible under the edge of her windbreaker. Her head rested on a blue, tubular pillow, and her face was partially covered by a lock of black hair and the collar of her jacket. Her eyes were closed, and a fly crawled across her cheek.

He had seen her before. They had talked about a dog and music. And now he wondered why she slept so close to the trail and did not awaken when he approached. Modesty told him to pass by, but her inertness urged him to stop. Standing above her, he cleared his throat, but that did not stir her. Then dropping to a knee, he murmured, “Madame?” No response. Finally, in desperation he slid his hand up under the wind breaker until he felt her shoulder. He shook it with fearful gentleness. The gesture was useless. She too had begun the long atomic walk into eternity.